KV-116-265

I BN

1 1 0456194 4

SPECIAL MESSAGE TO READERS

THE ULVERSCROFT FOUNDATION
(registered UK charity number 264873)

was established in 1972 to provide funds for research, diagnosis and treatment of eye diseases. Examples of major projects funded by the Ulverscroft Foundation are:-

- The Children's Eye Unit at Moorfields Eye Hospital, London
- The Ulverscroft Children's Eye Unit at Great Ormond Street Hospital for Sick Children
- Funding research into eye diseases and treatment at the Department of Ophthalmology, University of Leicester
- The Ulverscroft Vision Research Group, Institute of Child Health
- Twin operating theatres at the Western Ophthalmic Hospital, London
- The Chair of Ophthalmology at the Royal Australian College of Ophthalmologists

You can help further the work of the Foundation by making a donation or leaving a legacy. Every contribution is gratefully received. If you would like to help support the Foundation or require further information, please contact:

THE ULVERSCROFT FOUNDATION
The Green, Bradgate Road, Anstey
Leicester LE7 7FU, England
Tel: (0116) 236 4325
website: www.foundation.ulverscroft.com

THE MAN ALL AMERICA HATED

In the aftermath of World War Two, Alec McCrae is the most hated American anywhere: he acted as intelligence officer for the Japanese and tortured American prisoners, sending thousands to forced-labour gangs. McCrae has managed to elude his pursuers for six years — but when he and his associates are finally exposed and confronted on a flight bound for Australia, he causes the plane to crash-land on a deserted Pacific island. And if the fugitives are to remain free, they will have to murder all the surviving crew and passengers . . .

*Books by Gordon Landsborough
in the Linford Mystery Library:*

POISON IVY
FEDERAL AGENT
CALL IN THE FEDS!
F.B.I. SPECIAL AGENT
DEATH SMELLS OF CORDITE
F.B.I. SHOWDOWN
MAKE IT NYLONS
FORTRESS EL ZEEB
LEGIONNAIRE FROM TEXAS
RENEGADE LEGIONNAIRE
BACK TO THE LEGION
THE SPAHIS
THE GRAB

GORDON LANDSBOROUGH

THE MAN ALL AMERICA HATED

Complete and Unabridged

LINFORD
Leicester

First published in Great Britain

First Linford Edition
published 2020

Copyright © 1952 by Gordon Landsborough
All rights reserved

*A catalogue record for this book is available
from the British Library.*

ISBN 978–1–4448–4375–0

Published by
F. A. Thorpe (Publishing)
Anstey, Leicestershire

Set by Words & Graphics Ltd.
Anstey, Leicestershire
Printed and bound in Great Britain by
T. J. International Ltd., Padstow, Cornwall

This book is printed on acid-free paper

1

The Man All America Hated

They were a thousand miles beyond Hawaii, Australia-bound, when things began to happen. The big four-engined Constellation was eight thousand feet above a sun-drenched blue Pacific when the light went on for'ard, calling the stewardess.

It went off and on, off and on, quickly. That meant someone was in a hurry. It was a pity that stewardess Josie Melita didn't see it. Josie was pretty level and could take things without excitement, but she was back in the galley, pouring out long drinks.

Etta Hersch — Peaches — saw it. She was being pleasant to the glamour girl when the light began winking, and Glamour didn't like it when she went off with only a quick 'Excuse me.'

Peaches was such a nice-looking blonde it was probable she was basically blonde at that, and most men like the natural type when they're as nice as Peaches, even personnel managers. Which was why she'd got the job. But she didn't have the savvy and steadiness that brunette Josie Melita had.

She went forward and closed the door behind her, then came out a few minutes later looking excited, though she was trying not to show it. For a few minutes she came along, talking to the passengers — they hadn't many, this trip — but she didn't seem at ease, her natural self. She gave the show away, anyway, when she came to the man marked on the passenger list as K. Arthur King.

Because she stared at him, excitement brightening the brown eyes that weren't usual with that lovely blonde hair, and when he said 'No' to her — 'Would you like anything to drink, sir?' she foolishly repeated herself, as if unable to take her eyes from him. He was stiff in his seat as he watched her go back into the nose of the plane, where the crew were.

The plane droned on, seeming not to move in that cloudless sky. It was just the right temperature up here in the speeding Constellation, and the other passengers were reading and talking, or were back in their tip-up chairs getting some sleep.

There was no hint of tragedy at that moment.

Then Peaches came back, and, she couldn't resist looking again at K. Arthur King as she passed. Just one quick glance, but it wasn't the kind of look a trained stewardess gives a passenger, certainly not one who has his wife with him.

Peaches couldn't wait; she was bursting to tell someone. Josie came out with a tray, very trim in her white tropical uniform. Peaches tried to stop her, but Josie slipped by and gave the drinks to some suffering luxury-travel passenger, and then returned, tray held against her skirt. She said humorously: 'Now what, petal-brain?'

Peaches got dramatic and started in round about. 'You know what, Josie? We just got a radio from 'Frisco. That big fellow out there — K. Arthur Someone. Guess who he is?'

Josie was impressed. 'You tell me — quick.'

'McCrae — Alec McCrae!'

Josie didn't get it. You don't, not always. If someone had said 'Dwight Eisenhower' it might have been the same, with Josie having to start thinking: 'Now, I've heard that name before . . .'

So Peaches interrupted impatiently and mouthed in exasperation: 'Alec McCrae! *The* Alec McCrae! The one all America's been looking for since the end of the war!'

And then Josie's mouth opened. 'McCrae!' The most hated American anywhere. The man who had acted as intelligence officer for the Japanese and tortured American prisoners — the man who had sent thousands to death and worse in the forced-labour gangs. The man who had backed the wrong horse and ended up a bad loser.

McCrae had disappeared at the capitulation of Japan, but he had been hunted the world over by outraged Americans. Not even Hitler was hated as much as the renegade. But somehow he had managed to elude his pursuers — six years after, he was still at large. Now Peaches was saying he was here, on this plane bound for Australia.

4

'McCrae,' Peaches was saying again, bobbing her pink and white face to give emphasis to the words, and then she looked beyond Josie and her expression became horror-stricken. 'My God,' she whispered. 'The guy's coming towards us!'

If she hadn't given the game away by now, she certainly did when she saw K. Arthur King heaving his bulk between the swaying seats towards her. Josie turned, and for once she didn't know what to do.

King was without his sunglasses for the first time on the flight. He carried them in his hand, swinging them like a bent twig in his fat white fingers.

He was a big man, but, you didn't realise his height until you stood against him because he was so solid with fat. He wore a lightweight gabardine summer suit, light grey and well cut.

He had a big, flat leather face that said he was about fifty, but it might have lied by as much as ten or twelve years. Fat faces are like that. You didn't see much of his eyes because of the folds of flesh, and his mouth was a long line across his face that spoke of a rye-and-cigar-tainted breath . . . In fact, he looked just like a prosperous Wall Street financier.

He looked only at Peaches. He said, 'I'm pretty good at lip-reading. I was watching you. Now, what was that name you were mentioning just then?'

Peaches went close to Josie. Suddenly he looked to have strength, and there was a hidden note of ruthlessness in the way he spoke that made her heart bump.

K. Arthur King said, 'It started with Mac, didn't it?' The women didn't answer. Josie was trying to see beyond that fat grey arm towards the first of the passengers. Someone was rising. Her hopes lifted, then fell. It was the glamour girl coming back to the powder-room. Josie wanted a man.

K. Arthur King said, 'You said McCrae — Alec McCrae, I think. Now, tell me what this fuss is about.'

Glamour girl came up. She was the tennis girl of the century. When she stepped into a court she was a fashion parade in herself, and no one was interested in her tennis. But she could play; she was devastating with her serve. She was good and she knew she was good and she let everyone know how good she thought herself to be. The stewardesses had been cheesed off with her long before they reached the Hawaiian Islands, though the male members of the crew seemed to have stamina for this kind of punishment.

She came up now, murmuring a brief, 'Pardon me,' and began to push her fine athletic form past the fat man.

Josie said quickly, 'Get the captain quick, Miss Van Kass!'

But Esther Van Kass didn't tumble. She wasn't used to doing things for other people, certainly not for airliner stewardesses. She carried on another yard, and that put her past K. Arthur King. The big man then moved across the gangway, and that trapped the three women up by the galley and powder room.

Esther was about to enter the powder room when K. Arthur King said, 'Just a minute, Miss.' Josie suddenly saw that he was sweating, and there was strain on his face. Esther turned. He was taking a hip flask from his pocket. He said to the star tennis player, 'I want you to step inside the galley for a minute, miss. I want all you three together.'

Josie said, 'I don't intend to go into the galley, Mr. King. Please step aside — '

K. Arthur King said, 'Look, made in Japan,' and touched a button and the flask split in half. Inside was a tiny automatic. He took it between his fat fingers. He didn't point it directly at them, but he didn't need to.

Esther Van Kass went up-stage at once. 'What's the meaning of all this? I want to go to the powder room — '

K. Arthur King started walking forward. He seemed to bundle the three women over the threshold of the galley and then he slid the door to. He said, 'Now you can scream. No one'll hear you.' They knew he was right; no one would hear them above the noise of those powerful engines and the slipstream that flowed over the streamlined cabin. They just stood and looked at him, a big, fat, well-dressed city man with an absurd little gun in his hand.

King said again, 'Now, come on, what's all this McCrae talk about? Why did you come staring at me, a while back? You can't kid me, lady; I knew you had something on your mind.'

Peaches looked sullenly across at Josie, as if it were her fault. Her slim nyloned leg was gawking out, doodling patterns on the rubber flooring with her neat shoe. She had courage — more courage than discretion, perhaps. Suddenly she came out with the truth: 'You're Alec McCrae. We just got a signal from the San Francisco police. They've traced you to this plane under the name of K. Arthur King. They wanted to check to make sure you had the physical resemblance to the Alec McCrae they're after.'

'So they sent you out to check up? It was this cyst at the back of my right ear you had to look for, wasn't it? I could feel your eyes looking hard at it, and that really gave the game away.'

Peaches began to get tough. 'So what? They'll be waiting for you when we land in Australia. Better go in and get drunk before the mob get at you and tear you into lumps of grease.'

McCrae's fat face showed that he didn't like such talk. But he had things to do, quickly, and the women could see that he was thinking desperately.

Suddenly he seemed to have made up his mind, for he waggled the little gun threateningly and said, 'You women stay in here; if you follow me through this door, I'll blow a little hole through you where it won't do you any good. Understand?'

Big, athletic Esther Van Kass woke up then and started forward angrily. 'You big bastard,' she said, 'threatening me with a gun!'

McCrae lifted his hand and then seemed to let it fall by its weight alone. It slapped into Esther Van Kass's face and she fell between the two stewardesses. Both immediately went down on nyloned knees to help her. McCrae slipped out and closed the door behind him.

He walked forward until he came to his seat, then he sat on the arm-rest so that he could look back towards the galley door. He beckoned, and his wife knelt up

10

so that she could hear him. Her hand flew up to her throat. She was another big woman. She was a blonde, too, but for all the good it did her it might as well have stayed in the bottle. She was thirty-eight, about, and getting tired in a lot of places all at once. Nona McCrae had big raw-boned shoulders, so that it looked as though she'd forgotten to take the clothes hanger out, and big heavy-boned thighs, and she was flat in between. She was no beauty, but might have had looks when McCrae first found her, back before World War II.

She had slipped off her shoes to rest her feet, and now she started to put them on, but McCrae snarled at her and she went quickly forward without them and spoke to two men who were sitting apart. They seemed just as startled, and one began to argue, but she left him and they came up to where McCrae was balancing his bulk on the arm-rest.

They hadn't many passengers, this trip — nine all told. A losing proposition to the Australasia-American Airways. But it gave plenty of room for McCrae to hold his conference, right there in the middle of the Constellation.

McCrae pulled out some octagonal-shaped rimless eyeglasses and fitted them on before speaking to the two men. Then he opened his hand and let them see the gun in it. He looked down the gangway to the door of the galley, gently opening, and said, 'I don't understand it. For five years . . . more . . . I've stayed safe in hiding. My first trip out, this has to happen.' He repeated himself bleakly, 'I don't understand it.'

He let his eyes come back to his two male companions; the woman — his wife — he ignored altogether. She was used to being ignored.

One of the men was thin and dark, with a pain-lined, sallow face and quick, unnaturally bright brown eyes. The brightness wasn't due to humour or intelligence. It was fear . . . and worry. He couldn't keep still, and now he moved his hands and then his feet and then he said, 'I think it's Nona.'

Nona McCrae looked up. She was trying to stuff her foot into her fashionable shoes. She seemed frightened at the thought, afraid to be blamed. She said quickly, 'That's silly. What do you mean, Joe?'

There was a resemblance between the two, Joe and Nona. If he'd used peroxide on his hair — or she'd let hers come out the colour at the roots — the resemblance would have been much greater. They might have been brother and sister . . . they were.

Joe kept shuffling around and then said, 'Don't you see, Alec? Maybe they've been watching all the time for Nona. They wouldn't recognise you — not after all these years, like this. Not unless suspicion was directed against you. But if they had got a line on Nona . . . '

Alec McCrae didn't nod, but they knew he accepted the theory. Nona went on quickly getting into her shoes, face flushed from having to bend, her movements showing panic that grew.

Joe seemed to give way to panic, too. He grasped the slack of his shirt in front and groaned, 'Oh my God, this is starting my stomach again!'

Josie had opened the galley door and was standing there, watching. The other passengers hadn't stirred at all; they didn't know what was happening.

The little man who stood with McCrae was in grey also. Altogether he was a grey little man. His hair was mostly grey, though he couldn't have been much over forty; his skin had the grey look that comes from a long sojourn within walls. He, too, wore rimless eyeglasses. They had a curious effect on him — you couldn't quite see his eyes through them, so that, as Alec McCrae had once remarked, you felt that he had blinds over his eyes. That way you can't get through to a man's mind, not if his eyes screen it from you; you have a feeling of blankness, remoteness . . .

Suddenly he started talking. He was a practised talker. He said, 'My case is complete. I have nothing to fear. I was coerced into helping the enemy, and if I did speak for them it was because I honestly and sincerely thought that that way I would be saving the lives of my countrymen. I have nothing to fear, and

14

when we land in Australia I shall quite voluntarily give myself up to justice.'

McCrae turned to look at him pityingly. He said dispassionately, 'How you talk! But you only kid yourself, and that not too well, otherwise you wouldn't have stayed in hiding with me all these years.'

'You know why — ' The small grey man was in his stride once more. McCrae interrupted him. He could be brutal, McCrae, even in the way he interrupted someone else speaking; but that was the only effective way of turning the tap off.

'Charlie, you haven't got a hope in hell. You'll get justice — you'll get what comes to people like you! You'll fry, so why kid yourself?'

Josie had come a few steps down the gangway, but she wasn't certain. In the galley doorway was Peaches, and she wasn't coming a step beyond. No, sir, not with a man sitting there back of a gun.

The man in grey was prepared to argue. 'I dispute it. And what will be your end, Alec? They hate you far more than they hate me — my God, don't they just!'

McCrae had finished thinking now. He took a case off the rack and opened it. He said, 'They won't get me, Charlie. D'you think I'm going on to Australia, knowing what'll be waiting for me?' He took something out of his case. 'Customs aren't so smart,' he said. There was another little automatic in his hand now, and some clips of ammunition.

The grey, stiff little man said quickly, 'You've got an idea, Alec? I should have known. What is it?'

McCrae didn't tell him. He slipped the automatic across to the small man saying, 'Take hold of this. We've got to act quickly now.'

But the grey man shook his head and said, 'I've got one in my coat. I've been carrying it ever since we were smuggled out of Japan. I'll go get it.'

McCrae turned on his wife's brother and shoved the automatic into his hand. 'Do something useful,' he growled contemptuously. 'To hell with your stomach for five minutes. You're in on this up to your neck, you know. What'll they say when they find my wife's brother's been hiding America's number one hate all these years? And taking plenty dough for it?' There was a grating humour in the big man's tone. It wasn't pleasant.

Joe Gunter turned abruptly, lips twitching. 'And what about my stomach? That's what I've got for it all. Hiding you and worrying, worrying, worrying. Getting more and more involved. And growing ulcers every week. Oh God, if I'd my time to come over again!'

McCrae said, 'It won't come. And if you don't do as I tell you, your time on earth won't be protracted, either. Look, I'm going forward. I know this part of the world; I flew over it soon after Pearl Harbor. I'm going to talk to the pilot about it. I think I can work things.'

'What do you want me to do?' Gunter's face was haggard, because he knew.

'Kill anyone who makes any move likely to endanger us. And that goes for that woman down there. In fact, kill her first, because she looks dangerous.'

2

Crash Landing

His wife was pathetic. She was terrified, but her terror seemed even now less for the situation in which the party found themselves than for fear of the man she called husband. At this moment she had to ask a silly question — trying to please, and only drawing danger upon herself.

She said, 'Alec, what do you want me to do?'

He didn't speak, but there was contempt in those eyes back of the rimless glasses.

Incongruously, Nona McCrae started to powder her face with a trembling hand. And then she started to cry. Life was over for her. It had really ended that day over five years ago when she'd gone into hiding with her unexpectedly returned husband.

McCrae walked forward; behind came

the little grey man, eyes blinking behind his glasses. His lips were moving. He was talking to himself, justifying actions past, present and future. That was his way — to use words; and when he used them he could put up arguments that proved black was white to quite a lot of people, including himself.

Gunter was left sitting on an arm-rest, the tiny automatic out of sight under his arm. Josie went back to say something to the other women, and the door closed behind her. Gunter stirred and seemed relieved.

The radio officer/navigator saw the door open and McCrae come in sideways. His eyes went wide, because he knew who McCrae was now. He half-turned, and then McCrae was against him, the small automatic held almost touching the operator's face.

It was noisier here, in the nose of the big plane. Perhaps for that reason, McCrae didn't speak; instead he jerked the plug cords out, tore the headphones off the operator, and trailed his automatic through the valves. He didn't mind hurting the man, either.

McCrae jerked over his shoulder, 'Don't let anyone touch that radio, Charlie.' And then he went a couple of paces forward. The captain and first officer were at the controls, the latter with his leg swung over the arm-rest. Because of the noise and vibration from the four powerful engines, they hadn't been disturbed.

But the engineer officer had. Rather late in the day he began to understand. He was engaged in picking the bits out of a salad that had come up on a tray earlier; then he saw the movement to rip off the radio officer's headphones and he came jumping across.

McCrae just shook his head and pointed the automatic. That stopped the engineer. He knew what an automatic was. McCrae jerked his head, and the engineer stepped to one side and raised his hands as he saw he was now being covered by the gun in the little grey man's hand. It looked bigger, more formidable, in that smaller hand.

McCrae tapped the first officer on the

shoulder, and he came out of his seat fast.

The Norwegian was at the controls. Everyone called him 'the Norwegian', though he was sound American stock by a couple of generations. He was a six-footer, lean and scrub-haired. A calm man, because only calm men are picked to fly trans-Pacific airliners.

He looked up, saw the gun, and his eyebrows brushed. 'What the hell game are you playing?' he demanded, his voice lifting above the roar. Then he looked at the first officer and said, 'You take over, Pat. I'll deal with this son of a gun!'

McCrae reached out and shoved the first officer back a couple of paces. He had strength in his arms, and his heavy face was hard. He said, 'Just try to get out of that seat, and I'll put a bullet right between your eyes. You know how much good that'll do you.'

The Norwegian hesitated. Pat Rorke gave a little signal for him to stay where he was and not risk anything. So the captain stayed at the controls.

But he could talk. He said, 'You're McCrae.' The big man didn't answer. The

Norwegian's voice was contemptuous as he looked at him. 'You're a bit heavier than when you were flying Forts for Uncle Sam. I wouldn't have known you. Your pictures don't look like you anymore.'

McCrae said, 'That was the idea of putting on weight.'

The Norwegian looked at his panel and then turned again to McCrae. 'You went into hiding, and you ate and ate until you got like this, and then you came out pretty sure no one would recognise you. That disguise must have taken some years to put on — and in the end someone did see through it.'

McCrae said, 'When you've finished talking . . . ' He didn't lose his temper; that was why he was so dangerous.

The Norwegian kept on flying and said, 'Yeah? What? When I've finished talking, we'll be touching down in Australia, and there'll be a lot of people out to meet you.' McCrae didn't say anything. The Norwegian said, 'Only they'll never get you to the hot seat when they take you back to the States, McCrae. A lot of people who hate you more than anyone's ever been hated in the world before — they'll take you out of any jail that's built, and they'll get you and they'll pull your limbs off one by one and you'll die just as you sent thousands of your countrymen to die — in awful torment.'

McCrae stood brooding over him, his face unemotional. He was listening, wanting to hear. Because it was novel, hearing an opinion that wasn't Joe's or Charlie's — all he had heard in over five years. His wife? She never gave an opinion. She never had one, now.

The Norwegian was getting vicious, sitting up there at the controls. He said, 'And you know what? I'll be right there with them.' He leaned forward; he wasn't scared by the gun at that moment. 'D'you know why? Because some of my boys got shot down in the Rickenbacker raid — you got hold of 'em, and we know what you did to 'em, too. I want to see you die like that, the way you set your men to killin' those boys.'

McCrae started to speak. He began it by levelling the gun at the Norwegian. He said, 'You've talked enough. What you say won't happen. First, I'm not going to Australia; second, you don't think I'd let myself fall alive into the hands of my democratic countrymen, do you? And if you want a third point, I'll kill every goddam American who stands in my way to freedom.'

The Norwegian said, 'And you ain't kidding.'

McCrae looked swiftly out through the glass nose and saw the blue sea far beneath them. He said, 'We're not far from the Tahao group of islands. I worked things out back there. Some of those islands had emergency landing strips laid down. We could land on one of those strips.'

The Norwegian turned contemptuously and didn't alter course. McCrae leaned forward and suddenly shouted, 'By God, you'll do it, Captain, or your second pilot will do it for me!' The Norwegian knew what he meant.

Pat Rorke came forward and said truculently, 'Who says I'll do it, you blasted renegade?'

McCrae said, 'Okay, okay. If you don't do as I say, I'll shoot the pair of you — the lot of you. And I'll take the plane in myself. After Forts, I suppose I could handle a Constellation. Maybe not many people would stay alive the way I'd land it, but I'll take the risk myself. Now what do you say?'

The Norwegian sat and looked forward for about a quarter of a minute, and then turned to look at Rorke. They didn't speak, but perhaps they understood each other. So then the Norwegian turned and said, 'I think you mean business with that gun. Okay, I'll find Tahao.' He started to swing north, and McCrae's face creased into a slight smile. He knew what the Norwegian was thinking. One slip and that lean, hard young Constellation captain would be at him.

The Norwegian was playing for time. McCrae didn't intend it to be of any use to him. He knew what was going to happen to everyone when they landed. He was beginning to think that some good could come out of this scare . . .

The radio officer had worked out a

bearing and now passed it over of the captain. The Norwegian altered course again. They were flying with the sun on their port beam now, and it was descending; it was coming late into the afternoon.

Twenty minutes later, the Norwegian nodded forward and said, 'Tahao.'

McCrae said, 'I'll take your word for it. Now bring her in to land.' He didn't take his eyes off the captain and first officer.

The Norwegian lost height and circled. He said, 'By jeez, but that strip's gone to hell. It's made of broken coral, and the rains have made holes in it the size of a house.' He turned angrily on McCrae. 'We'll never make it all in one piece,' he said.

McCrae ordered, 'Make it. I don't give a damn how you do it but — make it!'

Pat Rorke said, 'Those people back there should be warned. They won't stand a chance . . . '

'Just switch the light on, saying 'Fasten belts.' That's the only chance we'll give 'em,' ordered McCrae. 'And now — you . . . all of you lie on the floor. I'm having no tricks when we come in to a bumpy landing.' Slowly, he himself eased down into the second pilot's seat. But he didn't take his eyes off the captain.

The Norwegian said, 'I'm going in this time. But I don't like it.'

He banked, came straight, put down his flaps and lowered his undercarriage. They were losing height rapidly, coming in slowly. Sea rushed to meet them, then a foam of white surf, then the yellow strip of golden beach, then palm trees — then they were on to the end of the short runway.

When they touched down first time, they bounced twenty feet up off a hole, and then they came down again heavily and went bouncing along. They were losing speed, but not fast enough; and then the starboard wing tipped and scraped the ground and started to crumple. Desperately the Norwegian gunned the starboard engines to prevent them from crashing round in a small circle — and partly succeeded. And then they ran into the sandy beach at the end of the track and stopped, heeled over on to the starboard wing.

The Norwegian rose with blood coming from his split lips, but McCrae, wedged into the seat, waved him back. The rest of the crew were scrambling to their feet; the little grey man appeared to have been knocked out by the sudden landing, but McCrae kept the four men covered.

He shouted, though the engines had stopped and there was no need to do so, 'Get up, Charlie. Goddam it, can't you look after yourself!'

'Charlie?' said Pat Rorke, turning his grey eyes towards the little man, getting up. 'Birds of a feather . . . Now, that wouldn't be Japanese Charlie, the Radio Renegade?'

The radio officer, a plump man from Oakland, said nastily, 'You bet you're right, Pat. He hasn't got fat. It's him — shouldn't I know? Monitoring that non-stop voice of his for a year for the Navy. That's two we've got, here.'

The Norwegian was getting over the dazed feeling now. He swayed again to his feet, shouting, 'What the hell's everyone standin' talkin' for? Get everyone out — quickly! There's gasoline runnin' down

28

that wing and it might ignite any moment.'

McCrae was backing to the door. He said: 'It's an idea,' but he didn't mean what they thought he meant. From the door he said, 'We getting off here. You can do as you like. But listen. We'll be right outside. We have guns and you haven't. Show your faces at the door for half an hour and I'll make holes in them.'

The Norwegian started forward. 'By God, you can't keep us trapped in this place! We wouldn't stand a chance if a fire started.' He looked down at the crumpled starboard wing; there was a curious dancing haze above it. That would be the gasoline evaporating in the hot sunshine. It was getting warm already in the airplane.

McCrae only said, 'You heard,' and shoved the little grey man through the door behind him. He closed it carefully. Almost immediately it opened and Pat Rorke stood there. McCrae didn't bother to fire, but went on retreating down the gangway between the seats.

The place was a shambles. Hand

luggage and coats had come tumbling from the racks when they landed, and now lay burst open and strewn over the seats. Joe and Nona were sitting together looking worried.

Josie was attending to the be-glassed middle-aged American woman who had been so disliked all the way up to now. She must have had money, because she wore good clothes, only they didn't suit her. In fact, no clothes would suit her. She was the kind that depressed good clothing — she looked a sack in anything . . . a shapeless, formless woman of advancing years, unloved and unloving, thought Josie.

Glamour girl and Peaches were still up by the galley. They had the door open but they didn't come out. Glamour was pretty shaken by the blow, but she was getting back some of the venom that character-ised her tennis. Peaches was having to say something to her and hold her back. You don't knock front-page stars around and not get reaction.

McCrae wasn't hurrying. He was doing a lot of thinking. He'd got the door open and stood with his back in the space. Hot sunshine poured in. The plane was beginning to be uncomfortably hot already.

Suddenly he jerked his gun towards the galley and said, 'You two, get all the food and water and drop it overboard.' They didn't move. McCrae said, 'Okay; you go see they do it, Joe.'

Joe went aft, holding on to the backs of the seats because the plane was heeled at quite an angle. The Norwegian had pushed past Pat Rorke in the doorway and was marching as firmly as a sloping floor would let him straight towards McCrae. The fat man in the well-cut grey suit slowly lifted his gun and pointed it. He didn't speak.

Pat Rorke grabbed his chief and held him. 'For krise sake,' he said, 'you won't do any good by getting killed. Hold on.'

The Norwegian said again, 'What the hell, this plane might go up in flames any moment. Let the people off, McCrae. You're here; what more d'you want?'

McCrae just said, 'The fire hasn't started; when it does, we can start

31

considering it. Meantime, I want you all where I can see you. So — shut up!'

His gun swept the other passengers: the American woman trying to hide back of the trim white-clad hostess; the old Australian who had had trouble at customs and had been mumbling to himself ever since; and the two men forward — one young and thin and not so healthy-looking, the other a British colonial servant, unassuming for all his high rank, quiet and courteous, the perfect passenger.

The British civil servant said very clearly, 'I don't know what you expect to achieve by all this. These islands are deserted, and you'll be picked up some day when some vessel pulls into Tahao. What good is that going to do you? We'll be on hand when you're picked up.' Then he straightened suddenly. He was looking up into that flat face; he seemed to have caught some expression there, and it disturbed him. 'Or will we?' he said.

Harry Carley, the radio officer, came through the door just then. He looked hard at McCrae and then muttered to his chief: 'He did a good job. I still haven't got a signal off. It might take me a few hours to get on the air again. Meanwhile — ' He jerked his head towards the crumpled starboard wing, with its constant threat of sudden conflagration.

Peaches and the dark, pain-ridden Joe Gunter came out with some containers of water and food. McCrae said: 'Drop 'em into the sand, then you go out with them. You won't hurt. Get the stuff well away from the plane, and then stand back and watch the emergency door on the starboard side. Anyone that shows his face, you kill 'em — quick. Understand?'

Gunter's face twitched and he half-closed his eyes. His breathing was heavy, and it wasn't from lugging the food and water containers. He whispered, 'Oh my god, my stomach'll never stand this sort of strain. I need a doctor.'

McCrae had no pity in his eyes. He said, 'You're no better than that sister of yours that I married. Get out!' with the loathing of a strong, ruthless man in the presence of a craven. Then he called to his wife, 'You follow.'

She said 'Yes, Alec' quickly, nervously, and came tumbling along with her arms full of coats and hand luggage. She seemed terrified of him, desperate not to earn his displeasure. And he liked it that way.

That left McCrae and Japanese Charlie. McCrae said, 'You can shut this door after us, can't you?' to Peaches. The soft-faced blonde nodded, but she did it surlily. McCrae said, 'Right; you stand in the doorway here beside me, see? When we leave you're goin' to close the door after us. Charlie's going out now, and he'll cover you from the beach while I drop out. If you don't shut the door, Charlie will shoot you.' His voice rose sharply. 'You will, won't you, Charlie?'

The man who radioed five hundred times on behalf of the Japanese during wartime began at once, 'In the circumstances, I'd be justified. We mean no harm to them, but in our position we cannot take risks. There has been a — '

McCrae bit out, '*Shut up!* Goddam it, do you have to justify everything to your conscience? Get outside.'

Charlie teetered on the edge and then

dropped the eight feet or so into the sand. The Norwegian was restless. He shook off Rorke's hand and said, 'What in hell's the idea, McCrae, shutting us in this place? It's going to get unbearably hot — '

McCrae interrupted, 'You're right there, Captain. But you're in no position to demand answers to questions. Just stay put, all of you; if anyone shows a face when I'm outside, I'll blow another hole in it. And I mean it, in case anyone has other ideas.'

He glanced down quickly. Little grey-haired, grey-faced Japanese Charlie stood below, eyes screened by lights reflecting on his glasses. But the little gun in his hand was steady as it pointed up at the graceful figure of Peaches Hersch. Charlie wouldn't hesitate to trigger it off.

McCrae nodded, satisfied. But his bulk was too great to risk dropping out. He went on the floor, then slid his legs into space. Suddenly he was round on his stomach, but the hand that held the automatic came up in a quick covering movement. Rorke and the Norwegian stopped their simultaneous rush. Josie screamed, thinking someone was going to get killed. But

McCrae just slipped over the edge, held on for a second with his hands, and then subsided easily into the soft sand. The crew came quickly to the doorway to look down on the passengers below. It looked vivid in that sunshine, as they stood against a background of brilliant yellow sand — like an over-coloured photograph, Rorke was thinking.

McCrae came climbing clumsily up, his feet slipping in the fine dry sand. He had his gun pointing at Peaches and he said, 'That woman can't move faster than a bullet, so she'd better not try it. Now, I want that door closed. Get it closed. If you don't do it without argument, I'll shoot her. Do you want that to happen?'

Rorke sighed and reached for the long lever-handle. He said, 'So what? We can always open it again. It can't be locked from outside. And Peaches looks better alive, I think.'

The door came across. The Norwegian said, 'Yes, Pat, but what's he up to? How long are we to stay in here? That man hasn't a conscience, remember.'

He turned and started to go forward,

then he changed his mind and looked out through a starboard window. Joe Gunter was below; he was eating a biscuit. He seemed drenched with emotion, his face more lined and haggard and working than ever. He was in a bad way. All the same, when he saw the Norwegian's face appear high up at the window, he jerked his automatic significantly. Joe Gunter couldn't justify anything to his conscience, but he seemed desperate enough to open fire if he had to.

Then the Norwegian eased his long, supple body down between the seats on the port side and looked out. Back where the crushed coral runaway ended, Nona McCrae was standing with coats and luggage and containers all around her nyloned legs. She seemed as distraught as her brother, but she didn't dare say anything. The grey little man was standing well away from the plane, too; he was facing it, gun ready, curiously detached, as if far away in his thoughts.

The Norwegian said, 'My God, the swine!' And that brought everyone to the windows.

McCrae had rolled a bunch of grass into a crude rope; he was holding his cigarette lighter to it, trying to set it aflame. It would flare up and then burn out; he kept on trying, but that was all that happened.

Rorke shouted, 'The fool! He's too near that spilt gasoline. Does he want to set us on fire, playing out there with his lighter . . . '

His bronzed face came swiveling round in horror, his eyes meeting the Norwegian's. The big fellow just nodded, and then both went tumbling forward.

The Norwegian said, 'We'll get shot if we show up at the doors.' He looked out towards the starboard wing. Big McCrae had approached it and was dipping the grass bundle into the stream of gasoline that flowed steadily down the wing. He walked away with it. The Norwegian sat down at the controls, saying, 'I haven't a doubt now, Pat. McCrae means to set fire to the plane and burn us all to death!'

3

McCrae Must Kill Us

Perspiration was streaming down Rorke's face. He said, 'That's what I was thinking. What're you goin' to do?'

The Norwegian said, 'Get everyone up by the doors. I'm goin' to try to get the plane moving down the beach out of range of their automatics. We might catch fire as soon as I start the engines, so be ready to bail out, all of you. It won't hurt.'

Rorke said, 'But you, up here — '

The Norwegian roared, 'Go on, Pat! Don't argue!' and started the nearside starboard engine. Then the nearside port engine roared into life.

McCrae's startled face turned upwards; he dropped the bundle of grass and started shooting. Some glass developed myriad-tailed white stars, and then the plane gave a lurch forward.

Rorke was shouting instructions, dragging

people towards the doors. Harry Carley, quick for all his plumpness, took up station by the port-side emergency door — the engineering officer pulled himself across to the other.

The roar of the engines suddenly deafened them, and then they were thrown across the floor as the big plane lurched gallantly against the resistance of a wing trailing in sand. Nothing stayed in the racks now; no one could stand upright for an instant. Everyone was rolling into each other; no one could hear the shouts of fear and pain and blind anger.

But they were moving. And the Norwegian was fighting to keep the craft on a straight line, striving to lift the broken wing a little by gunning the starboard engine. He was watching it as it dug a deepening furrow in the soft sand.

And so he saw the renegade, still smart in his businessman's grey suit, come across in slow-motion fashion, grass torch blazing, and hurl it on to the gasoline-covered wing.

There was a whoosh and a roar as the

starboard engine fanned the flames like a blow lamp. The entire wing was ablaze and the engine with it.

Desperately, because he knew they had only seconds left, the Norwegian gave the Constellation the gun. Somehow the gallant plane got going at speed down the beach . . . fifty yards . . . a hundred yards . . . two hundred yards . . .

They were out of effective range; there was brush cover within yards. Rorke didn't need to be told what to do. All the starboard side windows were cracking from the heat of the raging flames against them. But what he was afraid of was that the tanks would go up any moment.

He shouted, 'Get out, everyone!' and flung open the door. The other doors opened. They were moving at speed — perhaps fifteen or twenty miles an hour. The heat was terrific, and oil smoke came pouring in as the starboard emergency door was flung open. Jay Key, the engineering officer, slammed it to and clawed up to where Harry Carley was standing.

Pat Rorke grabbed the tennis star and

said, 'Out, Glamour!' and pushed her. She caught her balance and jumped and went down in a parachute of expensive summer frock. There wasn't time for order — Peaches was there and she went out without telling. Josie was dragging the middle-aged American woman across. The woman was screaming and fighting — out of her mind at that moment.

Rorke coughed up some smoke and reeled, almost falling out as they hit a bigger than usual bump. He shouted, 'Go on, Josie,' and Josie jumped. Rorke grabbed the woman, who had suddenly begun to crumple. There was no time for niceties; he dropped her onto the sand below.

Everyone seemed to be out of the plane. The old Australian had just stepped overboard grumbling, most casual for an old man. Then the pale young man. It was hard to see against that cloud of smoke. Rorke didn't know what the position was, exactly.

And then the wing erupted, just as the engines died down.

Rorke found himself blown out through the door; found himself falling. He had an impression that little Jay Key came out, all arms and legs, from the emergency door up forward, and he wondered what had happened to Harry Carley and the Norwegian.

He didn't feel the landing, but there was sand in his hair when he sat up and it came trickling down his face. He looked first at the plane. Black smoke was roaring up in the draught caused by the flaming gasoline. The plane had stopped twenty yards farther along; the flames were blowing back into the plane and across it. Within two seconds as he sat there, it seemed to leap afire from end to end . . .

'The chief!' he shouted in agony, swaying to his feet. The Norwegian was in there, up forward. And then he turned. He couldn't look at it. Because that fine, calm captain of theirs must still be alive inside it, yet without a chance of survival. He couldn't do anything for him down here.

There were people out here who were alive and had to be protected. That was his duty. Harry Carley was only a couple of yards from him, thank God. And Jay Key was standing, horror on his face, looking towards the plane.

Rorke shouted, 'Don't stand there. Get under cover. She'll up any second!'

He looked round. Far down the beach was the big grey form of McCrae; behind him the others. They were hurrying towards them. Rorke shouted, 'Run for it — McCrae's after us!'

Peaches, Josie and Glamour were on their feet. Josie was crying, looking at their lovely plane, knowing what was happening inside it. Peaches didn't understand. All three went stumbling towards the palm trees and the brush. Jay Key gave a hand to the old Australian, but the pale, ill-looking young man, surprisingly, ran strongly and was easily first into cover. Harry Carley got his plump legs into action and thumped a heavy way across the sand.

Rorke remembered, looked swiftly round and saw the almost indistinguishable bundle among the coarse grass roots. He ran frantically across, aware that McCrae was coming nearer every second.

It was the middle-aged unlovable woman. She didn't move. Rorke started to drag her, but after half a dozen yards he stopped, bent over her, and then suddenly left her and ran after the others.

There was a sharp crack down the beach, but the bullet didn't come anywhere near him.

He crashed through among the shrubs. Now he was suddenly conscious of the heat, realising that he was wet with perspiration. The others were strung out in the brush, but they were making a lot of noise, and all were working in towards each other.

Rorke started shouting to bring them together. But he kept on steadily, pushing his way through the luxuriant grasses and flowering shrubs, putting as much distance between them and the beach as he could.

They closed in. Rorke counted them. Except for the Norwegian, all the crew were there. Glamour came up, getting angry because all this had happened to her. And the thin young man and the old Australian.

Rorke rapped, 'We're one short — that Britisher!'

Little Jay Key lifted a sweating, agonised face. 'Oh my God, we must have left him in the plane! I never saw him towards the end. I thought he was up with you.'

Rorke said, 'And I thought he was with you. But he wasn't moving, when I got blown out. He must have got knocked unconscious when we were being rolled around the floor.'

Harry Carley cleared his throat. He was trying not to show emotion. He was inclined to be emotional at times, though calm enough on his radio job. He whispered, 'My God, being fried in that plane! Even unconscious. And the Norwegian . . . '

Rorke looked quickly at the stewardesses and said, 'Forget that, you dope.'

He started to move on, deeper into the island. Jay Key said, 'We've forgotten that woman passenger. I thought you were bringing her in, Pat.'

Rorke said, 'I was. But then I found she was dead, so I left her.'

'Dead!' Even Glamour was shocked by those three sudden tragedies.

'Yeah. She might have died up in the plane, I don't know. Or I might have killed her, pitching her out.'

Josie tried to help him. 'I think it was in the plane, Pat. I remember the way she went down. Don't blame yourself — '

Rorke said shortly, 'I'm not. There wasn't anything else I could do.'

The Australian said, 'Well, I'm going to take my collar and tie off. I've had enough for one day.' Only he said 'gowing' and 'tike.' And he took off his collar and tie, and looked suddenly very homespun. He was an old man, probably approaching seventy, brown face lined with years, but sturdy. Rorke looked at him and thought, *This old boy's got sand in him. He won't be a passenger on this trip.*

Somewhere way back, they heard someone crashing through the bush. Rorke got his breath back and said, 'Look, keep in single file and close together. And don't make a noise. Let's make it as hard as we can for that bastard to follow us.' And as he thought of

McCrae, his hands clenched suddenly. By God, McCrae would suffer for this.

Rorke sent Harry Carley to lead the way. Harry just took them in a direct line with the sun that came filtering through the roof of palm trees, as far away from McCrae and his gun as possible. Rorke and Jay Key brought up the rear, with some vague idea of protecting the column. After a few hundred yards, Jay got the idea of smoothing their trail to make things harder for McCrae if he decided to follow them.

The ground was soft all over the island, and their foot-marks stood out clearly. When they began to wind among the tree trunks, the two airmen tore off branches from a kind of stunted palm and began to sweep the imprints out. It wasn't too successful, because it left the imprints of palm leaves, but Rorke thought that for a time it might be confusing.

The sun was straight in their eyes, low down on the horizon, when they came out on the edge of a lagoon. Only a few seconds before, as they were going through some thick brush, Glamour had to open her mouth petulantly and say, 'There aren't any natives or Japanese in these parts, I hope.'

Burke heard Peaches give a little gasp of alarm, and he said, 'For Pete's sake, glamour girl, don't start that sort of talk. Haven't we enough to worry about?'

Harry Carley turned and said shortly, 'Tahao's been deserted, I believe, since the atom bomb experiments — all the islands in the group.' And then they stepped out onto the narrow beach of the lagoon.

Rorke looked at the three women. He noticed that only Glamour was wearing shoes. He said: 'You saving footwear, Josie?'

She managed a smile. 'I lost mine trying to get across that beach with McCrae chasing us.'

Peaches said so did she.

And they looked tired. Unlike Glamour, those women had been working for the past eight hours. The old Australian didn't seem uncomfortable, though, and neither did the younger man, the pale, silent one.

Rorke said: 'We can't go on walking forever over this island. But very soon it'll be dark, and then we can hide up from those thugs.'

Jay Key mopped his balding forehead, and said: 'Why not just sit tight here, Pat?'

Rorke nodded. 'That's what I was getting round to, Jay. Let's get down in these bushes — don't anyone show up on the beach — and if we lay quiet we should hear that blundering elephant if he comes this way. Just another hour and we'll be covered by darkness.'

They sank down inside some thick bush, thankful for the rest. They had come fast, over tiring ground; now their limbs wanted to recover from the exertion. They talked in whispers, all except the old Australian, who put a handkerchief over his face and seemed to go off to sleep.

Peaches said tearfully: 'It was horrible in that plane, just before the end. Why did he do it? Why had he to try to burn us alive?'

Rorke stopped wishing he had a pint of cold beer and said: 'I don't know. I haven't had time to think. Let's work it out.'

Jay Key rolled on to his elbow and spoke. Jay was spare and undistinguished, but he was a pretty good engineer, and he was sharp. He said: 'Don't you see? They're waiting for our Connie in Australia — a nice posse of police, I reckon. When we don't come, they'll assume another mysterious air tragedy — they'll think we've crashed.

'Some day someone'll come to Tahao and see that burnt-out Constellation and will assume it is ours, will assume we were forced down through some trouble or other and just burnt up. That is, if we're not around. And that's why Traitor McCrae wanted to burn us all up — so that we wouldn't be around.'

Rorke looked up at the feathery palm leaves, silhouetted against the deepening blue of the evening sky. He was wondering how long it would be before he couldn't see them . . . then they would be safe for a few hours.

He said: 'And McCrae had . . . has . . . the idea that if we are out of the way, if the authorities think we all perished in the wreck, the hunt will end for him.'

'That's it.' Jay Key sat up and wrapped thin arms around bony knees. His uniform white pants were ripped around the bottoms and no longer very white. 'He's got some idea back of his brain that he'll build a boat and get away in it. Anyway, any plan's better than sitting tamely in a plane that's taking him into the arms of the police. You know, the way American people are right now, I can't see him ever coming before a court . . . '

Rorke said, softly: 'I used the word 'has' a minute ago, Jay. Didn't you get what I meant?' He turned his eyes round to meet Jay Key's grey ones. Jay thought a minute, and then nodded, his face showing his thoughts. Rorke said, so that the others couldn't hear: 'Shall we tell the others, do you think?'

Jay sieved some dry sand between his fingers, and then asked: 'Why not? It's their lives he's after.'

So Rorke sat up and said: 'Look, folk, you must face up to facts. McCrae and his friends can't leave us alive on this island. They've got to hunt us down and kill us to the last one, otherwise the pack will still be after them. If they can kill us and dispose of our bodies, in time they'll be able to get away from Tahao. They'll be presumed dead, at any rate when the burnt-out Connie is discovered, and so they'll be able to start their lives anew with the past washed out.'

Radio officer Harry Carley took out his empty pipe and said: 'Like hell he will. Not if I can help it.' He wasn't soft, Harry Carley.

Rorke turned to him. 'That's just it, Harry,' he explained. Rorke was the natural leader after the Norwegian. He was a big man, though young; the biggest man in the party, and big men generally command and lead. 'That's why I'm telling you all this. I'm trying to impress upon you all that this man isn't fooling, and he'll go on hunting us until he gets us — or we get him.'

'Or escape.' That was the old Australian's contribution from under the handkerchief. A dry, thin, nasal-Cockney Australian comment. He was a cool old boy.

Rorke said: 'Well, now you know. For God's sake, be careful . . . And now be quiet, so that we can hear if Gutsy McCrae is on our trail.'

There was silence as they lay, warm and comfortable, on the hot sandy earth just back of the beach. Peace everywhere, but not in their minds. Each one was busy with his or her thoughts, and there was no comfort in them. It was chilling, frightening, to think of that man hunting them relentlessly back there in the bush.

Josie suddenly crawled across on all fours and then lay with her head pillowed on Rorke's chest. She had had enough; she needed comforting. Those tragedies — especially the end of the fine, likeable captain — had shocked her; she took it harder than the superficial Peaches.

Rorke pulled his head up and saw that her face was white and trembling a little. She had good features. She was a good woman. Rorke gave her a wink but didn't say anything; he put his hand out and she took it in hers and lay there clasping it hard.

Rorke turned back to look at the sun through the bushes. It was halfway below the horizon. Just now it was their enemy;

for the moment, McCrae would be able to see their tracks by it, could see them. But in half an hour the light would have failed and they would be safe until the sun rose on another day.

Well, that'll be something, he thought. *A night's rest gives us a better chance.*

He turned to look at the lovely lagoon, about a quarter of a mile wide at this point. There was a small island a hundred yards offshore with a solitary coconut palm on it. It looked very small, perhaps no more than thirty yards in diameter. Rorke was beginning to think about that island.

Peaches came sliding across, and now she, too, pillowed her head on Rorke's chest from the opposite side. Rorke grinned and stroked the fusion of soft, dark hair with the brilliant blonde tresses. He whispered: 'I know. I've got personal magnetism.'

But Peaches just moaned: 'My God, Pat, you should see my nylons — ruined!'

Rorke mentally threw up his hands in despair. The feather-brain could think of nylons at a time like this.

Glamour sat up, big and blonde and beautiful in her thin summer dress without sleeves. She said: 'Does the crew get all the comfort on this trip?' And Rorke couldn't be sure whether she was being humorous or faintly annoyed. He decided there was something of both in her tone.

He drawled good-humouredly: 'If you can find a place, join in. I'm thoroughly democratic, Glamour.'

And then he sat up abruptly, disturbing both the stewardesses. For the big blonde tennis star said nastily, 'Miss Van Kass to you, please. You don't speak to passengers like that.'

Rorke heard Harry Carley say, 'Well, if that doesn't beat everything!' And a dry, rasping chuckle floated up from under a handkerchief. The old boy thought that was good, too.

Pat didn't let it get in his hair. He wasn't the kind. He had calmness sufficient for half a dozen men, and tact for twice that number. He said sorrowfully, 'Honey, there are no passengers on this trip now. And I'm damned if I'm goin' to give you that mouthful every time. If you don't like Glamour, Esther it'll have to be.'

She pouted even at that, and didn't like it. Because she was the great Esther Van Kass, ranking No. 2 in American tennis stars, and she couldn't forget it, not even here, with a man gunning for them.

Rorke just let her sit and get mean by herself. He shifted and placed his back against a palm trunk and let the women settle down comfortably again. He was stroking their hair; there wasn't anything nicer, more soothing, than having your hair gently stroked — or stroking it.

Then he saw that the tall, pale passenger was fidgeting and seeming to get worked up about something, and finally he got up and walked a dozen yards away and sat stiffly erect looking out to the red reflection where the sun had disappeared.

Jay Key was watching him, and he said, 'What the hell's biting that bird? Something is.' And there was a curious memory back of his mind of an unhealthy dog that used to have fits and do sudden unaccountable things.

Rorke looked at that stiff, slim back and said, 'God knows,' frowning.

The old Australian came up out of his handkerchief and squinted between his dandy pointed shoes and then turned his wrinkled prune of a face and said with rasping humour, 'Oh, him. His mother's eatin' him alive, that's what.'

4

Prestowe Sets a Problem

Peaches looked up and said the first thing that came to her head. 'I don't get it.'

The old Australian dropped his voice to a whisper that couldn't have been heard more than fifty yards away — not much more. He was the soul of tact.

'Confidentially, I'm travellin' with him. We come from the same part of Sydney, an' his mother wrote and said would I come back with him; I'd be company for him.'

He went through the motions of spitting in the sand. Rorke grinned. The Aussie was an engaging old boy. Then Rorke went back to calculating how many more minutes of daylight there were left.

'Him,' said the Aussie contemptuously. 'He don't smoke, he don't drink, he don't believe in gels. *He don't even swear!*' That was the limit. 'I came back on the plane

with him, but I was damned if I was goin'
to sit with him. What'd we have to talk
about?'

Rorke pricked his ears. He thought he
had heard a foreign sound in the distance.
He wanted to say, 'Quiet for a minute,'
but Peaches came up with, 'What did you
mean, his mother was eating him alive?
That sounds interesting. How long will he
last?' Which was quite a bit of humour
from the blonde stewardess.

And the dry old voice was explaining,
'Don't you know the kind? Widowed
mother with one chick, and she's
determined she'll never lose him to
another woman. Only she don't openly tie
him to her skirts. She goes around
looking very frail and old, and she works
herself to death for him. So he thinks
there's no one like mother, and he tries to
live up to the purity of her standards. You
know what I mean.'

Harry Carley said, 'Sure, I know what
you mean.' Rorke had relaxed. That noise
hadn't come again. 'Possessive mothers
who won't let their children lead natural
lives. It's subconscious with most of

them; they don't know what harm they're doing. But they do harm.' He looked across at the erect figure.

The old boy had a piece of grass sucking between his thin wrinkled lips. He said, 'He thinks worldly pleasures are sinful. But back of him he'd like a taste — it's only natural to want pleasure when you're his age. So when he sees you with an armful of women, it makes him mad and jealous, and he has to go away and not tease himself with the sight.'

Peaches said again, petulantly: 'Is that all you meant when you said she was eating him alive?' She was disappointed.

Rorke said, 'He's a problem child. He might make trouble for us; they often do.'

The light was fading rapidly — another five or ten minutes and they could count themselves safe. A couple of minutes passed and then Rorke started slowly away from the trunk, his body stiffening. Startled, the women pulled themselves into a sitting position.

Rorke said, 'Not a sound.' Because he had heard a stealthy movement back in the bush. They all sat up, straining. Rorke

61

was looking across at the young Australian — what was his name? Prestowe, John Prestowe.

Then they all heard something breaking not too far away. Someone was approaching, coming along slowly. Perhaps following their trail. Another minute or two and there wouldn't be light enough for that; even now it must be very difficult.

But it was too late to start running; the only way they could go was along the beach, and that would present them as targets for McCrae's gun.

Rorke whispered, 'Prestowe, come back and lie down. You're silhouetted against the skyline.' He waited. Obstinately the man didn't move. He waited another second and then realised that Prestowe didn't intend to come back. And that put the whole party in danger. He heard another sound, still approaching.

He thought, *That guy's so full of frustrations and repressions he doesn't know what the hell he's doing half the time.* But he had to be made to do as he was told.

Jay Key was already going forward on hands and knees, and Rorke went along with him. He had a feeling that someone else was coming, too.

Rorke snaked up to the man. He looked to be about twenty-six, quite a good-looking fellow . . . the artistic type.

Rorke said, 'Come on, fellow. You don't want to get us all in trouble, do you?'

Prestowe deliberately didn't look at him. He sat, very pale and obstinate, and Rorke thought, 'Sure, chum, you don't want to take orders from me because you've just seen me with two nice women in my arms — you think women are sinful, but you'd love to have an armful yourself, wouldn't you?' Only his mother always stood in the way of such thoughts.

Rorke didn't know what to do. Force would only attract attention. And who-ever it was who was coming nearer wasn't far away now. And there was still a little daylight.

Esther Van Kass shoved her much-photo-graphed face indignantly into Prestowe's. It was Glamour who had followed. She hissed, 'Come on, you young fool,' though he was older than she, and she grabbed him by his coat collar and pulled.

Glamour did it. He couldn't fight against a woman. He was on his back near to the others before he knew what had happened, his face turned, hating himself for being shown up as weak when he had tried to assert himself through obstinacy.

Someone came up, slowly, heavily. They heard hard breathing, heard the bushes parting, the dry grass crackling underfoot. Coming nearer. Almost on top of them. But it was nearly dark.

They saw a bulk loom against the sky over the lagoon, followed by a much smaller, straighter shadow. That was the trouble. There might have been a chance of jumping McCrae alone and getting his gun. Then they would have had nothing to fear. But they couldn't jump two gunmen simultaneously, safely. Not from a dozen yards.

That was how near McCrae and Japanese Charlie came to them. And then they went out onto the beach and they heard McCrae growl something about giving it up for the night, and then the two men with guns trampled heavily down through the sand along the beach.

When they had gone, everyone started to breathe again. For the first time, there was even gladness in the party. They had gained a respite; anything could happen in the next few hours, and it might be in their favour.

Rorke said, softly, 'Now, everyone get to sleep. But the first to waken around dawn must waken us all, understand?' He had a plan developing.

Josie and Peaches snuggled down in his arms. It was flattering, very nice, but tiring. When they were both asleep, he lowered them to the soft sand and dropped off himself.

The warm night breeze stirred the palm leaves and chafed them together with a dry whispering sound; the water in the lagoon washed gently along the edges of the nearly white sand beach, still warm from the day's sun. Stars came, and a moon rode up thin and crescent-shaped after midnight.

And all the party moaned uneasily in

their sleep and dreamed of water. Except the tough old Australian. He slept with his mouth open and wallowed in gallons of beer from a Sydney brewery.

Glamour was first to move, though not first to waken. John Prestowe had been awake for hours, trying not to think of the three lovely women sleeping so near to him. Obstinately he wouldn't waken Rorke; that was the last thing he would do. So Glamour did it.

She came over to where Rorke lay between the two quietly sleeping hostesses and said, 'Come on, Sultan; wake up.' And her tone was midway between humour and annoyance again. She liked to be the centre of all attention and she was missing it.

She stood up and stretched in the grey morning light. She was a mighty creature, with her strong-muscled legs and broad, strong shoulders; yet womanly, graceful, attractive. And she said, 'I'm off for a swim. I feel terrible.'

Rorke said, 'You'll have a swim, but not just now.'

He was on his feet, watching the first

red rays of the sun creeping back of them through the palm trees. 'Get everyone awake,' he ordered. 'But no noise. We don't know how far that murderin' so-and-so is.'

Jay Key came up, yawning, to say, 'My guess is he's back on the runway. They wouldn't lug those food and water containers far last night.'

And Peaches moaned, 'Food and water! Why did you have to mention it, Jay, you microbe!'

Rorke called them together. 'I want to move before McCrae gets around again. But listen, I don't think it's any good chasing up and down this island in front of him. I don't believe this island is very big — maybe a mile or two long at the most, but probably not more than a few hundred yards wide at its widest point. If I know McCrae, he'll start a systematic drive down the length of the island. In one day he'd get the lot of us.'

Harry Carley said, 'That's a bright prospect. But you've got an idea, Pat. What is it?'

Rorke was worried. 'I'm not sure my

idea's a good one. Last night I was looking at that little island out in the lagoon, and it occurred to me that it might be a good hiding place for us for a while. I mean, somehow you wouldn't think of hiding in a place so tiny, so exposed, would you? I think McCrae will probably go past it, at any rate the first time . . . ' His voice trailed off. It was a responsibility, and he wasn't sure.

Jay and Harry Carley and the old Aussie went and looked at the island. Jay and the radio officer weren't so sure about the move, either, but the old Aussie said, 'It's your only chance. If it isn't taken, we'll all be dead mutton before night.'

So that settled that.

Rorke said, 'Walk in each other's footsteps across the beach. Jay and I will come last after we've wiped out all marks around this camp of ours.'

Glamour led the way. She was dying for a swim. Harry followed. Then the others. Hastily Jay and Rorke removed all traces of their night's stay and then went back down the beach obliterating the tracks.

Then there were seven in the lagoon, strung out, swimming for the island, Glamour well ahead, churning the warm green water in a fast crawl.

And one man watched them go and then walked inland . . .

Glamour got out and went and sat against the solitary tree trunk and watched the others come in. She didn't return to help them out, which was characteristic of her . . . Actually it just never occurred to her. Her dress clung wetly to her and she shivered and felt uncomfortable.

Prestowe came in next. He was a man of contradictions — he looked a cissy, but he seemed quite athletic. He came in fast, using an Australian crawl, though he wasn't exerting himself or showing off. He crawled out and sat away from Esther, but for some reason he made an effort to smile at her as he passed.

Josie and Peaches weren't in the Olympic class, and they were having difficulties as Rorke and little Jay Key came ploughing up. Harry Carley was helping them. Like many bulky men, he was pretty agile in the water. Harry called out as Rorke came up, 'They should have taken their coats off. It's thin stuff, but it's pullin' 'em down.'

Rorke spurted. He could see Peaches' agonised face. She was drinking water and getting panicky; her hair was in dark streaks down her cheeks, though still blonde on top where it was dry.

He said, 'You hold Josie; I'll take Peaches . . . Don't panic.' Peaches was fighting for breath, getting hysterical. It was a poor place to start things, a hundred yards off shore. Rorke went under as she grabbed and he had a vision of the pair of them being drowned; then he shoved hard and got her round, his hand cupping under her chin so that she was floating above water, talking urgently in her ear, 'For heaven's sake don't panic, Peaches. Keep calm a minute longer . . . We'll have you out of that jacket . . . I'll tow you in safely. Keep calm . . . '

And she did. Jay swam up and got her out of her encumbering jacket, then moved across to Josie. Josie was taking things quietly, just floating, while Harry

Carley kept her head up. She was a good woman, Rorke kept thinking; Josie kept her head.

He called over the dancing waves, 'Don't let the jackets go, Jay. Bring 'em with you.' If the jackets got washed up, they would attract attention to this part of the lagoon.

Harry and Josie got well ahead and were out before Rorke came steadily in with Peaches. Jay wasn't finding it easy, pulling the jackets and swimming with one hand, and he had drifted along the island quite a few yards.

It was deep water right until they hit the island, and the coral was sharp to their hands and knees as they came out. Josie and Harry were on hand and easily pulled the blonde stewardess out of the water, and Rorke came up unaided. Peaches had gone limp, and Harry turned her on to her face and started to pump up the seawater.

Rorke went along the island to give Jay a hand. He was looking east. The sun was rising, red and hot in their faces, but he was looking for a sign of McCrae and his party. If McCrae came out now, they would be trapped, sitting targets for his gun if he could get a bit nearer. But McCrae was probably half a mile up the island . . .

The pilot stood on the bank as Jay came in, balding head wet, face showing that swimming wasn't his forte. But grinning. The solitary palm had roots that held the soil together here, and they went out before descending into the water, forming an uncertain overhang. Jay was swimming across the front of it, only a yard away . . .

Jay was swimming with a root over one shoulder, his face opening into horrified panic.

Jay was swimming with roots round his neck.

Jay was screaming.

The roots were alive and moving.

Rorke found himself shouting in horror as Jay started to go under, and Harry Carley came crashing across to see what was wrong.

Rorke went flat and reached out. A waving root touched and then wrapped itself round Rorke's arm, and that saved Jay Key's life. Harry Carley was holding on to Rorke; the octopus was holding on to Jay Key *and* Rorke, and that kept Jay's head above water.

Rorke shouted, 'Hold hard, Harry,' and then let go of the tree root he'd been holding and reached out and grabbed Jay by the shirt neck. Harry Carley understood without telling. As soon as Rorke's hand was on the shirt, gripping, Carley took hold of Rorke by the forearms and heaved. He had plenty of strength — anyway, plenty at that moment, with death holding on to a comrade.

Screams of horror rose from the women a dozen yards away as a mess of limbs and black threshing tentacles rolled on to the bank. Rorke panicked as the cold, wet mess came across his body — and then his face. He fought himself free, and dragged himself a yard away.

Jay was shouting, held in the middle of those writhing sucker-faced tentacles. And then Harry Carley went jumping in, heels stamping down.

5

The Graveyard

Before Rorke could get in to help, Jay had torn himself loose. Harry was standing there, stamping up and down like a madman. And the tentacles were only thrashing now, not gripping.

Harry jumped clear, blowing. He said, 'That's a dead octopus if ever I've seen one.' And it was dying.

But Rorke was looking beyond, and now he said, quickly, 'Get out of sight, all of you. Someone's heard the noise!' Someone was moving through the bushes only a couple of hundred yards along the sandy-edged lagoon. Someone big.

He pulled the jittery Jay along, and everyone flopped on the far side of the island, out of sight. Jay lay by his side, his eyes closed, and his body racked by long shudders. After a while he felt better and opened his eyes and said, 'Oh, God, I don't ever want that to happen again! I'd sooner face McCrae!'

Harry lifted his head from the warm sand, his eyes twinkling. 'It felt the size of a house, didn't it? But you have another look. That's a little feller.'

Jay just said, 'Little or not, it would have done me no good if you two hadn't been there. Did I say thanks?'

Harry grinned and said, 'No, and it's about time. Saving your life. It's goin' to cost you something when we meet up with a bar.'

Glamour groaned, 'A bar! Something to drink! Even water. To think of all the drinks I've refused in my lifetime!'

And then Peaches turned a white, panicky face and said, her voice wailing, 'Oh, Pat, what are we going to do? We'll be stuck here forever now; I'll never dare go into that water again!'

The other women showed their horror at the thought, but Harry took a hand at consoling them. 'You can quit worrying,' he said. 'We're not likely to find octopuses swimming around — they don't do much of that — and there won't be anywhere that smooth sloping shore is. This island's the tricky place, but we'll find a way in that's free from long-legged folk. You see if we don't.'

The women looked unconvinced, Jay Key even less so. He'd had a nightmare. Harry tried to help by saying, 'The natives hunt them naked and without weapons, on some of these islands. One acts as bait and swims straight into the arms of a lurking octopus. That's to kid the brute. His pal dives down and yanks his friend and octopus from its moorings, floats both to the surface; then bites it between the eyes and kills it.'

It was Harry's way of being reassuring, to show how easy octopuses were. He looked surprised when Peaches turned away quickly and was sick. The other women looked white at the thought of biting an octopus to death.

Rorke grinned, 'Boy, are you the soul of tact!' And Harry Carley looked surprised.

Jay said, 'What happens if the octopus holds on down below?' He was recovering now; he was a tough little man.

Harry started to say, 'I reckon that's

one up to the octopuses,' but Glamour snapped pettishly, 'For God's sake, don't mention those creatures again or I'll be sick right over you, see if I'm not!'

Rorke came back from the top of the tiny island. He spoke quietly, because sound travelled easily over those still blue waters. 'Don't make any noise. McCrae's out on the beach. I'm not sure whether we got out of sight in time, and there's that damned octopus still kicking and giving the show away. I'll take another peep in a moment.'

Everyone sat still. Harry Carley could be heard talking viciously to himself. 'I wish that damned octopus had grabbed McCrae. I'd have sat there and enjoyed it and afterwards I'd have made a pet of it and taken it around Oakland on a chain. I'd have had a placard fixed on it saying, 'This octopus swallowed something that not even a hundred and fifty million Americans could stomach'.' And he went on talking.

There wasn't much wrong with Harry Carley's nerves. It probably helped to break the suspense of waiting. Waiting for a sound that would tell them they had been spotted and were trapped on a handkerchief-sized island in the middle of the lagoon.

Rorke looked across and saw that Prestowe was talking to Glamour. He didn't know what the fellow was saying, but suddenly Prestowe looked up and caught his eye and immediately flushed as though he had been detected in some weak act, and then he shuffled a couple of yards away on his bottom and sat stiff and silent once more.

Rorke thought, 'Oh my god, he's goin' to be a handful!' You couldn't predict how a balled-up fellow like that would react to any circumstance. Then he went off and peered over the rim of the island for a few minutes. When he came sliding back he was grinning.

'That octopus kicked itself into the water and now it's drifting away, just twitching a bit. And McCrae doesn't seem to know we're here. He's doing just as we guessed — he's walking down the beach, but you can hear the others strung across the point, moving in line. I'll bet it's playing hell with Joe Gunter's stomach.' That was some satisfaction.

He sat on his heels just above them, and then his thoughts came back. They were all looking at him. There was something queer, the way they were looking. He said sharply, 'What's the matter?' — knowing something was wrong, that tragedy was imminent. Because even Glamour was looking wide-eyed and chilled.

Harry Carley licked lips that were cracking for want of water. He said, 'We've just spotted something. We're a man short!'

Rorke looked quickly over them — all the crew were there who had come off the plane, Glamour, Prestowe . . .

'The old boy!' He nearly stood up in horror. 'What's happened to him? Where is he?' For a moment he had a vision of root-like limbs coming silently up through the water, closing on the tough old Australian and pulling him under. The old boy struggling, perhaps gasping out a shout that was lost in the general confusion . . . the poor old boy dying within yards of them, fighting unavailingly for his life in the grip of some cold-blooded under-water monster.

He whispered; 'Oh God, I hope it wasn't — '

Harry Carley stopped him quickly, before he put fresh terrors into the minds of the women. 'No, Pat. We've been talking about it. We think he couldn't swim — Prestowe says he's pretty certain he couldn't. We think he didn't come down the beach with us.'

'But it was the old Aussie that urged us to come here for safety!'

Carley bowed his head and played again with the sand. His voice was soft. 'We think the Aussie saw this was our only chance, but he couldn't share it because he couldn't swim. But he wouldn't hold us back, so he slipped away into the bush when we weren't looking. He's a game old boy, and as brave as they come.'

Rorke sat on his heels, listening. He said, 'He's back there and they're out gunning, and he hasn't a chance. The way they're strung across the island, they're bound to get him.'

He started to get out of his soiled white uniform jacket, and then took off his shirt and vest. Jay Key started to do the same, and Harry Carley was only a second after them.

Josie asked quickly. 'What are you going to do?'

Rorke said grimly, 'We've got to do something. We can't let the old boy die without trying to help him. And we'll swim faster without shirts and jackets.' Then he looked at Harry. 'You'd better stay with the others,' he said. 'We can't all go, and you're too big to go stalking quietly through the bush.'

Harry protested, 'You're a lot bigger,' but he knew what the pilot meant, and grudgingly he climbed back into his shirt.

They were ready. Rorke said, 'Look, McCrae will work round to the west prong of the lagoon over there, in time. You're exposed here. There's a depression along by the tree; start digging it deeper with your hands. It's sandy and it won't be hard. Then get inside and keep your heads down.'

Peaches lifted a woebegone face and said, 'Pat, you've got to do something about food and drink. We'll be crazy in an hour or so without it. It's terrible.'

Rorke patted her hair; it wasn't looking so neat now, but the hot sun had already dried it. He said, 'Don't I know how you feel. We'll do our best.'

Rorke said 'Ready?' to Jay Key, and they walked over to where they could see the way in was clear — no overhangs, no underwater cavern or grottoes . . . no lurking eight-armed monsters.

Rorke was poised, ready for a long plunge out, when they heard it — a sharp crack of gunfire, back on the island. Slowly Rorke's arms came down to his side and he turned. They were all looking at him, faces stiff with horror. He didn't speak but came over and sat with them, and then Jay Key came and sat down.

They knew what that single shot meant. McCrae or one of his bunch had come across the old Aussie. That was one less in their party.

Rorke thought back. There had been eleven of them, apart from the McCrae party, when they flew out that morning from Hawaii. Eleven — and now there were only seven. One by one, they had died — the fine, fearless Norwegian who had saved their lives by his quick thinking — and died in holding on to the controls to the last second. Then the courageous, dignified British civil servant; and then the greedy, petulant middle-aged woman, dowdy and unlikeable.

And now that game old boy, the Australian . . .

He thought, 'How long will this go on?' And he looked round at his companions and wondered who would be next to go. If wouldn't matter to McCrae which one it was, or whether it was a man or a woman . . . In the end he would try to kill them all, to the last one.

After a time he got up and said, 'Well, we've still got to get food and water, and now's our best chance, while they're going further up the island.' The Aussie was dead; they couldn't bring him back. They had to go on as if nothing had happened.

He plunged into the lagoon and started to swim round the little island. Jay Key came after him.

When they came round the sea end of

the tiny atoll, he saw a submerged bulk bobbing not too far away. He went rapidly around the island away from it. Jay Key went even more rapidly. That octopus might be dead, but neither felt like verifying it.

From the little island a row of faces watched as they swam across to the beach. Rorke was a strong swimmer, and he had to wait for Jay Key to keep pace with him. Together they crawled out of the water and over the hot, yellow sand; then, on the fringe of the green undergrowth, both turned and gave a quick wave and then plunged out of sight.

Harry Carley felt the depression that came with their departure. Rorke was a big, capable type of man, the kind that holds a party together without even trying to do so. Without him, the women felt lost and scared. So he made them start to work to forget the feeling.

They dug a long shallow trough, deepening and lengthening the depression that Burke had mentioned, until it was big enough to accommodate all the party. It didn't take ten minutes, because the soil was so soft and sandy.

Peaches didn't do much, and after a petulant, temperamental avowal that she wasn't going to do a damn thing, Glamour suddenly got going and did her whack. Prestowe worked well, and built up the walls very neatly, so that there was no danger of them collapsing on the occupants. Then he went out and came back dragging some green stuff which he stuck along the lip of the trench — it acted as camouflage to any incautious movement, and it also gave welcome shade. The sun was so hot by now that it made them feel sick.

When that was done, there was nothing to do except lie and wait. Time dragged. Talking was difficult with a dry throat, but Prestowe and Harry Carley sat together and talked agreeably for quite a while. He didn't seem to mind Carley, perhaps because he was older, comfortable in his personality, and apparently unbothered by the charms of the three very bonny women who were in their party.

Prestowe had a good clear mind too,

and liked books and music. He had wit and humour, and considerable natural charm, but just occasionally they entered into topics where he displayed a rigid, obstinate attitude, uncompromising and even supercilious. Carley found he liked the man, but he set him down as a bit queer in some of his ideas.

Peaches started to moan after a while. She wasn't putting it on, either. She had drunk a lot of seawater that morning, and she was feeling ill. Harry saw that she was becoming light-headed and he grew alarmed, but he didn't show it. He prayed for Rorke to come back — Rorke with a barrel of water. And then he thought, *How the heck's he goin' to get it across to us?*

It was worrying. He didn't like being in charge of the party. Rorke could have the job — anyway, Rorke would make a better job of it.

Glamour suddenly woke out of a doze to say to Prestowe, 'Look, couldn't you get up that tree and throw down some coconuts?'

Prestowe looked doubtful, but he said,

'I'll have a try. We shall have to do something soon.'

Harry rolled over on the hot baking sand and said, 'Now don't start climbing trees yet awhile. You'd stick out a mile. Hang on a little longer; Rorke's a cunning fellow, and my money's on him.' Then he thought of another reason. 'Besides, what's the good? Those coconuts are solid with fibre; we'd need an axe to split 'em open.'

Glamour rolled on to her back and said viciously, 'Let me get at 'em and I'd crack 'em in my teeth!' The idol of Forest Hills and Wimbledon had lost a lot of her noise, but she was showing up tough underneath.

They were taking it in turns to watch the beach for a sign of the returning pair. Of McCrae and his party there was no sign — they were probably moving towards the far end of the island.

Josie was on lookout. It was a lovely scene that she looked over — the deep blue of the lagoon with the white foam at the entrance where the sea milled in and out . . . the lagoon, half a mile long and a few hundred yards wide here at the widest point. And all round that glorious, inviting strand of nearly white sand, reflecting the hot sun so that at times it hurt the eyes. And back, crescenting round, broken only where the sea entrance was, stood the lofty, gently waving palm trees, and the unbroken green of the bush at their feet.

Blue sky, blue sea, golden sands, tall green palms — and delightful sunshine. What more could anyone wish for?

But Josie just wanted to see Rorke. Anyone could have the whole darned row of palms for all she cared. Just let her see Rorke — and Jay Key, of course. And if they had a barrel of water between them, then she'd appreciate the scenery a little . . .

Someone came so swiftly across the distant beach that she didn't see the movement until it was too late, with her heavy, drowsy eyes half-closed against the glare. Then he was in the water, swimming steadily towards them.

One.

Her heart stood still for a moment, and

then she recovered and called, 'Some-one's coming, but — ' A catch in her voice. ' — only one!'

Silently they crowded up and peered through the fringe of greenery that Prestowe had stuck along the lip of the trench. The sun was reflecting in their eyes from the sparkling waves, so that it was difficult to see the face of the swimmer until he was close in on them.

And then the sunlight reflected on a high balding head gleaming with sea-water, and they knew it to be Jay Key.

Rorke wasn't with him. Their hearts chilled at the thought.

Harry risked being seen and went down to help Jay in. He saw the little engineer coming in, face agonized at the thought of another awful struggle with an octopus. Harry was watching the water and he called, 'Take it easy, Jay. I can see from here and everything's okay.'

But for all that, Jay came out with such a splashing of water it must have been heard the length of the lagoon. He had a water bottle slung around his neck, and it wasn't the kind of bottle you got aboard a plane, Harry noted, and he wondered at it. But it looked to contain a quart of water.

He dragged the exhausted little man up into their hideout, and they sat around and waited for his first words. He erupted salt water, and then said, 'We've found a graveyard.'

6

Who Shot the Aussie?

When Rorke and Jay Key slipped into the cool shade of the palms on the main island, both knew what they were going to do. First thing was to get food and drink for the party; it was going to be a race against time, for McCrae and his party might come to this end of the island again at any minute.

Swimming, Rorke explained his plan, his ideas. 'Usually you don't find fresh water on these islands,' he said. 'Only after rain. Until we find a way of getting up at those coconuts, there's only one water supply available to us — that's the water that McCrae got off the plane. While he's hunting for us, he won't be dragging water containers around. My guess is we'll find Mrs. McCrae sitting on the containers back at the end of the old runway.'

They weren't sure of their way, and when eventually they came cautiously out onto the runway, they were halfway along its length. In the far distance they could see the wreckage of the Constellation sticking up among the sand hills, and they set off towards it, keeping within the fringe of the bush.

They were almost crawling on hands and knees as they got nearer, and then Rorke went down on his face, pulling Jay Key with him. He whispered, 'There's someone in that bush, by the palm with twin trunks.'

Cautiously they raised their heads. The pattern of sunlight through the vegetation distorted things. After a while, Rorke got the impression that he was looking into a face that was peering straight towards him from the thicket beyond. He went down, moved a few yards and lifted his head again.

It was no trick of light and shade; there *was* a face looking across at him.

He went down again, and began to circle. Jay started to follow, but Rorke said, 'You wait there. Two's too many.'

Jay got up behind some roots so that he couldn't be seen easily . . . and that face was still watching. There was a man in that thicket, he knew. But it was uncanny, the way he just kept on watching, not moving. Jay felt his spine go cold and gooseflesh twitched his skin.

Then he saw Rorke stalking through the bushes. Saw him gather himself for a spring and then go flying through the air. At the last moment he seemed to miss the man, and turned in flight and crashed beyond. And then he got up and crossed to a tree and stood for a second with his forehead resting against his arm. And the face still stared towards Jay Key.

Rorke walked forward, beckoning Jay to come out of cover. When Jay came up, Rorke said, 'It's the old boy, the poor old Aussie. All the time, I was stalking a corpse. I only recognised him at the last second. Thank God I didn't tangle with him.'

Jay had never seen him so shaken. But after a while, both went to see how the old man had died. Rorke turned him gently over. The flies were getting at him.

There was a mess on his chest. Rorke said, 'He was shot through the heart. That's something else for McCrae to answer for.'

They went on. They saw Nona McCrae when they were a hundred yards from her, unexpectedly. Jay was saying, 'Looks like the old boy had the same idea as us. Tried to circle round McCrae's party and get at the water. But they spotted him. He was game, that tough old Aussie.'

Rorke said, 'Shh!' Nona McCrae was sitting on a big container in the shadows of the palms, not more than a couple of hundred yards away. The way she sat there, hands tightly clasped, moving her head quickly, you could see she was dying deaths every minute, scared out of her wits at being alone.

Rorke stood in the shade and watched for quite five minutes, the shadows of the leafy bushes shifting in a smooth pattern across the brown of his strong naked body. Jay Key stood and watched, drooping in the heat, now and then smacking at a biting insect that flew onto him. When he was sure it was no trap and

McCrae and comrades weren't sitting back in the bushes with guns out and ready, Rorke started to move forward.

He came under cover until he was right behind the woman, and then he stepped out. Jay stayed back a few yards, keeping watch.

Nona heard a slight noise and her face came contorting round. She saw Rorke, big, hard-looking, face grim, seeming to tower over her. Rorke saw a fading, angular blonde woman near to death with fear.

She didn't rise. She hadn't the strength. She sat and fluttered her hands a little and moaned, 'Oh, oh!' several times.

Rorke saw a beaker by her side, a big one that had come from the galley. It was nearly full. Nona must have kept it by her for refreshment at intervals while the others were away. He didn't speak but picked it up. The lipstick on it didn't worry him a bit. He started to drink. It wasn't water. It was lime juice, soda water — and gin. But not too much gin.

He drank half, then handed the rest to

Jay. It felt wonderful. Just another fifteen like that and his thirst would be half gone. But it would have to do for now.

Rorke counted the containers. There were two food containers, and two much smaller that would contain water. Probably Joe Gunter had brought everything eatable and drinkable in the plane. It still wouldn't be much, on the last leg of their flight.

He looked in one food container — there was a little liquor in some opened, near-empty bottles, but it would be worth taking. The other container had some food in it, but it didn't look appetising and there was appallingly little. McCrae and party must have had a good supper and breakfast. He felt the weight of the two water containers. He judged them to hold less than ten gallons. For their party of seven, that was water for three or four days at the very most, and scant rations at that, in this awful heat.

He sighed and thought: *We'll be lucky to drink the last of it, with McCrae gunning after us.* Then he heard a slither through the sand and came wheeling, snarling, fist poised . . .

Nona McCrae was coming towards him. Her eyes were fixed on him, and they were desperate. She was crawling through the sand, her knees throwing up parallel furrows. When Rorke whipped round, she went back on her heels, but her face just couldn't register any more terror.

Rorke said: 'What do you want?'

She whispered: 'Oh, can't you kill him? Can't you kill Alec, please,' as if begging him to do her a great favour.

Rorke said: 'He gives you hell, doesn't he?'

Nona shuddered, and her head dropped on her chest. Rorke hardly heard her voice as she said: 'You don't know. Nobody knows. Only Joe, and he's got him, too.'

Rorke said: 'I'll get McCrae, if only for one thing — for shooting that poor old man back there in the bush.'

'But he didn't.' Nona was still on her knees, talking desperately, as if wanting to convey to him the extent of her husband's infamy, and yet not sure that words were adequate. 'Don't you see, it's Alec all over, that shooting. He made Joe do it,

97

my brother. Joe had to do it. Alec cornered that poor old man and held him there while Joe and Charlie came up. Charlie would have shot him, and then talked himself in the clear afterwards — but not Joe. Joe wouldn't have shot anyone, so Alec had to make him do it.'

'You were there?'

'Yes.' Nona stopped speaking for a moment and sat and rocked in misery. Then she told how it happened. 'I didn't know what it was; I ran up when Alec shouted to us. The old man was standing there, not saying anything. Alec said: 'You might as well watch this, Nona. He's got to go or we all fry. They've all got to go and then we'll be safe. Well, I reckon someone else can do some killing. How about you, Joe?'

'The old man said: 'Don't you boys get to quarrellin' over a little thing like that.'' Nona's voice broke as she remembered his courage. 'Then Alec said: 'You, Joe, you shoot him. Head or heart, take your choice.''

'And the old man was standing there, listening, all the time?' Jay Key had come

98

closer. They looked at each other. The skin was tight across the little engineer's face; Rorke knew that if McCrae were there at that moment, the little man would tear his heart out. He thought: *McCrae's not human. By God, give me a chance to get at him!*

Nona's voice droned on. 'Joe wouldn't. He was shaking like a leaf. He's in an awful condition, is Joe, what with his ulcers and his neurotic condition. He could hardly stand. Alec put his gun to Joe's head and said: 'It's you or him, Joe,' and my brother knew he meant it. He'd have killed him without compunction. So Joe pulled the trigger.'

'Joe shot the poor defenceless old boy just to save his own skin.' Rorke's voice was biting. He pulled Nona to her feet, almost shouting: 'You and him, why couldn't you have done something in the last few years? You had chances, plenty chances.'

But Nona said: 'There, you see, I knew you wouldn't understand. No one can understand until they've lived with Alec. He does things, and you don't know why he's doing them, and then afterwards you find out, and then it's too late. Do you know why he made Joe kill that old man? It wouldn't have bothered him to have done it himself.'

Burke said: 'You tell me,' while Jay Key urged: 'Come on, Pat; quit talking and let's get to hell outa here.' Jay was nervous.

Nona said: 'Joe had never killed anyone before. Joe wouldn't have shot at you, even though be carried a gun — not before. But now — '

'Now he's got to. Now he's got to do his darndest to kill us all, because he's a killer himself and will die if we get away and tell on him — or McCrae and Japanese Charlie tell, as they would.'

Pathetically, Nona McCrae seemed almost pleased. She said: 'There, you're beginning to understand now. That's just like Alec. He knew Joe wasn't willing, but now he's made him as dangerous a killer as himself.'

Rorke put the two square containers one atop the other. He was working out the best way of carrying everything in one move. Nona seemed glad to be able to talk, to be able to unfold her sufferings to some audience. She was saying: 'That's what he did when he got himself smuggled back from Japan at the war-end. It had been secret, our marriage — few people knew about it. And after he'd been shot down in that Tokio raid and turned traitor, I just went away and didn't tell anyone I was his wife.

'He found me through my brother. Rang him, didn't say who he was. Said he owed money, so Joe gave him my address.' Rorke was watching the green bush, wondering if it was wind that was making that purely local movement. Nona was talking on: 'Alec just stayed with me, knowing I couldn't turn my husband over to the police. Then Joe came and recognised him.'

Rorke relaxed. It was just wind. He said: 'Why the hell didn't he up and tell the police where America's big hate was? They'd have given him a medal for it.'

Nona shook her head. 'Alec bought time — he said: 'Give me a day and I'll give you a thousand dollars.' Joe was broke; he took the money. A day didn't seem important. But it was. Alec didn't go, and when Joe got mad he just laughed at him. He said he'd taken money, and America would lynch him if they knew my brother had been bought over that way. It gave him a hold over Joe, when he took that money, and one way or another he's strengthened his hold ever since.'

'Even to getting him to commit murder.' Rorke could think of other ways a man might have behaved, even if he was broke. But he said: 'Carry a water container in your right hand, Jay; I'll do the same, and see if we can balance these two damned containers between us.'

The containers were far heavier than the contents. They found it especially hard going across the yielding sand, though it got better on the firmer soil under the trees. When they were a hundred yards along the green fringe, just off the sand, Rorke thought of something and said: 'Drop everything for a moment.'

He looked back. Nona McCrae was sitting in the sand, not moving. Rorke called softly and she looked up; he beckoned, and after a moment's hesitation she rose and came stumbling across. She looked big and bony, almost craggy in the face, where the worry had thinned her down. She hadn't been glamorous when she stepped aboard the plane in California, but she'd looked a whole lot better than this.

Rorke said: 'Look, Mrs. McCrae, I don't want to be hard on you. We're taking your water supply. You'll know what that means in as little as two hours — by mid-day. Frankly, I hope to God your husband and his friends suffer everything possible, but you . . . Well, take a good, long drink now; you're going to need it.'

He made her drink a pint of water — that was far better than gin and lime — and while she was drinking, he and Jay Key couldn't resist a drink also. Then he shoved a packet of drying sandwiches into her hand and said: 'Take my tip and eat 'em now, before that so-and-so comes back and sees 'em.' And then they left her, not even saying goodbye for a second time.

They avoided the place where the old Aussie was lying; they walked as fast as they could, just within the cover of the brush parallel to the neglected runway. Halfway along it, Rorke said: 'It was about here we came out.'

They sat down for a rest on the containers, keeping sharp watch for McCrae and friends. But they heard nothing except the hum of insect life and the soft stir of the breeze among the leafy bushes. Rorke was thinking hard. He said, softly: 'If we could hide out for a few days, conserving our water, we might force McCrae into submission.'

Jay considered it, and then raised the obvious objection. 'Our little island's not bad as a temporary hiding place, but we couldn't last out several days there. McCrae would be sure to start suspecting it before long. Besides — '

Rorke said: 'You don't need to tell me. You were going to say, 'How the heck do we get these supplies across to our little island?'' He shrugged. 'We can't swim across with them, and if we've to swim across every time we want a mouthful of water, we'll soon be spotted.'

So they sat in silence for half a minute, just looking into the distance and thinking. Then Rorke stood up and looked into space, and said: 'You get up on this container, Shorty, and tell me what that looks like,' and he pointed into the bush right at the end of the grass-grown runway.

Jay stood up, looked, and said: 'It's a hangar — or what's left of it.

Rorke nodded. 'Sure. We should have thought of that — they'd have hangars as well as runways, wouldn't they?'

So Jay asked the obvious question: 'What good's that going to do us?'

Rorke shrugged. 'I don't know. But look, while I'm here I'm going to have a look-see up at that end of the runway and find out what's up there. Maybe we'll find a new hiding place for us.' He looked at Jay Key for a few moments, considering. Right at that moment it was imperative that they gave careful thought to all their actions; too much was at stake to slip up anywhere.

He spoke slowly: 'Jay, you'd better stay

here. Moving, you attract attention. As it is, in this bush McCrae could walk past only a dozen yards away and not see you if you kept down. I don't know, but he might by lying up in some bush and he'll see me moving.'

Jay said: 'I get it. Better one be shot than two.'

Rorke nodded. 'Our party's lost one member this morning already. So . . . you stay. If you hear a shot, try to get the party across after dark to have food and drink.'

He nodded briefly and went away, thinking: *My God, if they've to lie up there all this day without food or water, they'll go nuts!* But that was the sensible thing to do, with a killer stalking through the bush with a baby gun in his hand.

He went with elaborate caution, moving in quick little rushes from cover to cover, silently, pausing after every move so as to listen for hostile sounds, and hearing none. When he came to the end of the runway, he stopped.

There were buildings and hangars everywhere, though the metal was rusting and dropping, and the woodwork was paintless and warped and sagging. Buildings and hangars, a little town back there. But an obvious place for anyone to search.

The paths were weed-grown, and grass and other vegetable life were growing up through the twisting, rotting floorboards. It was uncannily silent; ominous in its deathly stillness. Rorke found himself shivering, just to see the place.

But he went thoroughly over the camp all the same, moving cautiously still, keeping always in the shadows, turning each corner only after stealthily peering round. He didn't want to run into McCrae now — not now when he'd thought of a chance of salvation.

Most of the huts were empty, but in some lay equipment such as webbing and some rotting greatcoats and a lot of rusting iron beds. But Rorke wasn't interested in such junk; now, feverishly, he was searching for something far more important, and he thought they would be here, and then the tables could be turned on the murdering McCrae.

But he didn't find any. He went through every hut, and in the end he was convinced that his hunch was wrong.

He'd hoped to find a gun — maybe a few rounds of ammunition. He'd been sure he'd find it — G.I.s always left such things around when they abandoned camp. But . . . there weren't any.

After his sudden high hopes, it was crushing. He stood out in the sunshine, sweating in the heat, and got his breath back, because he'd been holding it hard for a long time so as not to betray himself by his breathing. Then he remembered some water bottles back in a hut and thought of a way of using them. He went and selected two that were obviously new and unused and slung them over his shoulder.

Then he took one long last look around the place and began to get a few more ideas.

To get back, he came round behind the huts, because there wasn't much cover on the straight avenues between them. He hadn't been round this way before . . .

He said: 'God almighty!' and rocked on his heels.

He was looking at an airplane . . . a whole line of aircraft. And back of them was another line, and back of them another.

And behind was a row of jeeps and back of them some trucks.

And back of them was an assortment of radio trucks, amphibians, field guns — and even tanks!

7

McCrae Suspects the Island

Rorke said: 'That must have been stronger gin than I thought,' and then then shook his head . . . and they were still there.

Then he began to remember things. There'd been a picture on one of the magazines — *Life*, he thought it was — pretty much like this. A picture of a hole in some Burmese jungle, with millions of pounds' worth of war equipment rotting away because it wasn't worth salvaging; the cost of recovery was too great. Well, that must be the situation here, in Tahao.

The Tahao Islands had been stepping stones in the advance by the Allies towards Japan. They'd got the stuff dumped on the islands and then the war ended, and after that no one had time to recover the equipment until it was too late and it had rotted through exposure to wind, sun and rain. That looked to be the story of this Tahao dump, anyway.

Most of the planes were without engines. He guessed that those that were left wouldn't ever fly again. Then he got another idea and climbed into a Mustang, and then climbed out again, jubilant.

But he didn't go away immediately. His brain was racing hard. He went quickly along the end of the lines — the jeeps and trucks were U.S. — their engines rusted to hell, and their tyres rotted away. He was going on to the next row of vehicles when he caught a movement at the far end. He stiffened hard against an amphibian, the muscles of his stomach tightening until he felt sick, anticipating a shot.

But it didn't come.

He peered out. McCrae, in his grey business man's suit, was coming slowly towards him, the sun glinting on his glasses. Rorke looked again and saw movement beyond, and realised that Japanese Charlie and Joe Gunter were moving down between the farther rows of

111

vehicles, climbing up to look inside them.

Rorke looked at the array and thought: *They're gonna be thirsty by the time they're through with that lot,* and then quietly backed away.

He ran flat out along the runway, knowing it was safe, until he saw Jay wave to him from the bushes, and then he plunged in. He came crashing through, startling the little engineer. Jay said: 'What's exciting you, brother?'

For a moment Rorke could only gasp to get breath back in his lungs, and then say: 'I've found a graveyard, bud. Boy, it's the best thing I ever struck in my life! It's given me so many ideas I don't know where to begin!'

Jay said caustically: 'Graveyards give me only one idea. Now give, you big ape. Tell me what's buzzin'.'

Rorke sat on a container and said: 'As quick as I can. Up there is a deserted U.S. army dump. There's everything. Harry'll be able to build himself a transmitter — '

'What!'

'He will. All the parts are there for a clever boy like Harry. And I'm getting ideas for you, too.' He got up quickly. 'And look, Jay, everything's safe for the moment. McCrae's up their searching the graveyard. Now's our chance to beat it across to the island without being seen.' He unslung the water bottles. 'Do you think you can swim with one of these around your neck?'

Jay Key said he'd try. He knew how much they'd be needing the water, back on their little island. So Rorke quickly opened a water container, fixed the emergency pouring spout, and filled both water bottles. Then he got out a beaker and filled it and gave it to Jay, saying: 'Two quarts isn't much among five thirsty people. We'll take our share inside us.' He drank a quick beakerful himself and then stoppered up the container. Then he said: 'You go on ahead while the way's clear, Jay. Make sure that Nona doesn't see you, that's all. She's so terrified of that husband of hers, she'd tell where we are for certain.'

'And you?'

'I'm going to bury this stuff so McCrae won't spot it. We'll come back tonight for it — all of us. I've found a better place to hide away — up by the graveyard.'

Jay hesitated, not wanting to leave the pilot, and then he saw that Rorke's plan was the best. He turned and went, and as he turned he had an impression of a big deep-chested bronzed man digging frantically with his naked hands, scooping the earth up at an astonishing pace.

Jay set off at a great lick towards the lagoon. He paused at the beach to make sure Nona wasn't looking, and then ran across and into the water.

When he was out a few yards, he suddenly thought again of octopuses, and he was so scared he nearly drowned. But he had guts, that little man; he knew how badly they were needing this water on the island, and he kept on, octopuses or no octopuses.

He saw Harry Carley come out and call to him, but his panic grew the closer to that island he came. Afterwards Harry told him he came out of the water like a jet-propelled launch, he came out so quickly; but to Jay he seemed to be crawling slower than anything he had ever seen anywhere in his life before.

Then he was out, oozing water out of his mouth and nose and ears, and everyone was crowding round except Peaches, who was sitting in a kind of ditch, looking queer.

When Jay could speak a second time, he took off the water bottle and said: 'There's another one coming. Share this between you.'

Harry sighed his relief; he hadn't dared ask the question. Now he said: 'Thank goodness for that. When we saw you alone — '

'You thought old Pat had gone under?' Jay sat up and grinned. 'It'll need a lot to get that boy down. He's out there now in his element. You should see him go through those bushes. Boy, an Indian scout could take lessons from him. McCrae'll have to watch out, or Pat'll be up behind him and have the life choked out of his carcass.'

He stopped abruptly, remembering the poor old Aussie. Then Harry said, 'Now, quit talking in riddles and tell us all about this nice graveyard you're so excited about.'

Jay waited until they'd emptied the

bottle. Harry and Prestowe had just a lick, a moistener, so that the women could share the contents between them. It didn't seem much, but it perked them up wonderfully. Peaches suddenly came back to the living and was well again.

'Another bottle and we'll be fine for a while,' said Glamour. The international tennis star hadn't thoughts beyond a drink of water right then; they wouldn't have recognised her, back in her normal swank haunts. But she still looked good.

Jay sighed and turned away from her and said, 'The next bottle's to last you until after dark, so don't think you're on a picnic.' And then he told of Rorke's discovery, and the ideas the pilot had. 'He says there's enough stuff for you to build a transmitter, Harry.'

Carley's hand shook at the thought. He wasn't looking quite so plump today — but browner, a lot browner. He said, 'Oh boy, what I could do with a transmitter. I'd have the whole of the U.S. Air Force around within six hours, once I got a key tapping.'

Jay said, 'He's got something cooking

for me, too. That boy's full of ideas. Only he hadn't time to say what it was. Now, what could *I* do?'

But Josie, from the lookout position, was suddenly crying, 'He's coming. Oh, thank goodness, Pat's running across the beach, coming into the water!' — suddenly crying. Josie had done quite a bit of weeping since landing on Tahao, but the events had left her unstrung.

Peaches was crying, too. And then Glamour started. Esther Van Kass wept because Rorke was coming back!

Harry said, 'It's been hell for them, no water an' worrying. It's kind of reaction, knowing he's safe.'

Jay said, 'Nobody cried for me.' So Peaches came and hugged him to show they hadn't meant anything by it, and at that Prestowe got up and walked away. He was a queer bird, couldn't stand such things . . .

Rorke just came batting in as if he'd been for a cooler. Didn't make any damned fuss about octopuses at all — probably had forgotten about it by now because he was busy thinking of other things.

He came up grinning and unslung his

water bottle and told them to go ahead. 'We've got a long stay here — that's all you'll get until we move, after dark,' he told them, but already he was squinting at the cluster of fibrous nuts among the palm leaves above.

He said, 'I brought a knife with me, a good old army pattern knife that'll go through a coconut. All we need is to get up among 'em and shake 'em down.' He started unfastening the leather straps of the water bottles, and joined them together in a big loop. He was kidding, but they didn't know how far it went.

He said, 'Esther, honey, you're the fittest. You're gonna volunteer to climb that tree. You just walk up the trunk leaning back inside this loop of leather.'

Glamour took her lovely teeth away from the water bottle and said, 'When you talk like that, I just stop loving you.'

So Rorke said, 'Okay, Jay, you whip up. You're light; you can do it. McCrae'll be busy for another half hour for certain, I guess.'

Jay looked at the tree and then said, 'You want to get rid of me? Me, I couldn't climb so high with the help of a hover plane.'

So Rorke said, 'Well, darn it, I'm going up. I'm not gonna sit here and watch those things all this hot afternoon.' And he meant it. He'd have tried it, only they all held him back and told him not to be a dope.

Josie said, 'You're not going to risk your neck, Pat. We need you too much. It might be hell here, this afternoon, but I guess we'll be alive when the sun sets for all that. So — siddown, feller!'

And then Prestowe came quietly up and gave them another good reason. He said, 'McCrae's sitting out on the beach looking across at us.'

The way they folded up and went quiet was comical. It was like mentioning a bogyman to a lot of kids. The women looked scared, especially Peaches; the men just looked at each other and their eyes said, 'Now what?'

Harry Carley slowly heaved himself off the sand and climbed to the rim. He peered over the top for quite five minutes and then came down, dusting his knees.

He said, 'McCrae's out there, sitting like a big frog, and he hasn't taken his eyes off this island all that time.'

'You think he knows we're here?' said Rorke quickly.

'I'm not sure, but I don't think so. He's come out on the beach well away from where you and Jay crossed it.'

That was something. After a few more minutes, Harry crawled back and stuck his head up cautiously among the greenery. While he was keeping watch, the others sat mute and looked at each other.

Rorke saw with a pang how thin the women had got. They hadn't eaten for a full day, and this pouring sun had dried a lot of the moisture out of 'em, he thought. It was showing in their faces. Funny, but if they could get at half a gallon of water each they'd just fill out to about normal. That was the way things were here in these hot countries.

They kept to the shadow of the green branches that Prestowe had stuck up, but it was feeble cover against that intense, high-riding ball of fire. Already, within minutes of drinking a pint of water each, they had raging thirsts.

Harry Carley at last came sliding down to them. He said, 'The other two have just come onto the beach, Joe Gunter and Japanese Charlie. They're sitting together, looking this way and talking.'

Rorke said, 'I'd give a lot to know what they're discussing,' and then he sat up and said, 'Look, now's your chance to get cool. If you slip into the water they won't see you if you keep the island between you and them. Jay and I will keep watch and warn you if they move. We've had our share of swimming.'

The women said, 'Not on your life!' They'd rather fry than share that water with an eight-legged thing. And Harry Carley didn't jump for joy. But Rorke insisted; he had an ulterior motive — he'd never get them into the water after dark if they didn't prove their courage now. And it was after the sun had set that they would have to swim across to the new hideout he had spotted for them.

He went and showed them a tiny sandy bay, shallow and most obviously free from anything harmful. He gave the wink to

Harry, and he immediately caught on and stripped off his shirt and then went and lay in the shallows. You could see it was a blessing, that coolness to his hot, dry skin.

Then José went in and lay gratefully in the water, and then the others. Prestowe seemed to do a lot of hesitating, and then the inviting coolness won and he went and stretched himself and even dozed off with some scooped-up sand for a pillow.

Jay and Rorke kept watch on the enemy. They saw the three sitting and talking, and then McCrae rose, trailing his grey jacket, and slumped heavily up the beach into the greenery. The others followed, knees bent, shoulders sagging under the weight of the fiercely burning rays.

Jay said, 'They got tired of searching the graveyard. They've given that up. Now they're wondering where the heck we can be.'

'Yes.' Rorke's eyes narrowed, watching the sparkling waves on the intense blue lagoon. 'And now they're trudging off to Nona McCrae, to get some nice long drinks.'

He turned and started fastening the belts on to the bottles again. Jay was startled at the energy and said, 'What're you up to, Pat?'

Rorke said, 'Look at that sun. Those women'll be daffy if they've to stand another six or seven hours of it. I'm betting that McCrae and buddies are going right to one end of the runway. The water's buried almost at the other end. Okay, my guess is I can get across and be back with a couple of quarts before they start hunting for us again.'

Jay stood, a worried, unhappy little man. He tried to argue. 'Pat, we'll make it. And it's such an awful risk for you. Let's wait until dark. If the others knew, I'm sure they'd stop you going.'

Rorke said, 'Well, don't let 'em know I'm going.'

He slipped over the rim and stood on the edge of the little island. It was right by where the octopus had come out to the attack. Jay suddenly had a fresh bout of misgivings and called, agonised, 'Pat, how do you know this isn't a trap? How do you know they're not waiting for you behind those bushes?'

Jay stood watching him, poised for the plunge; saw Rorke hesitate and then give the tiniest of shrugs; and then he plunged far out, barely going under the surface and then settled down to a side stroke which wasn't interfered with by the bottles slung from his shoulder.

He saw Rorke's dark head bob towards the shore . . . watched him crawl out and then stand upright, and then go walking up the beach towards the greenery. The way he walked, tense, arms swinging a little stiffly, Jay knew that he was ready for any assault.

But nothing happened, at any rate within sight of Jay Key. After a few minutes, he slipped over to where the others were lying in the water and told them what Rorke had done. Harry Carley looked awfully worried and kept shaking his head and saying, 'He shouldn't have done it; we could have lasted . . . risking his life like that.' Josie and Peaches just sat and looked unhappy, and even Esther seemed perturbed. Prestowe went on lying in the shallows and didn't seem to hear them.

Jay thought, 'I wonder if that fellow would be glad if Rorke didn't come back? He doesn't like Rorke.' Why? He shrugged. Because Rorke seemed free and at ease in his relations with the women, and Prestowe couldn't be natural with them because of his repressions, and he accordingly hated — or was that too strong a word? — anyway, didn't like the pilot.

Jay thought. 'This is getting involved. Now, who started this tangle?' And then remembered it was Prestowe's mother.

When it was about time to expect the return of Rorke, they all came out of the water and stood silently watching through the fringe of greenery from their trench — all except Prestowe, who stayed where he was in the shallows.

No one spoke. No one moved. Minutes passed. A bird flew, nearly settled, saw them and wheeled away. And then Josie said quickly, 'Someone's coming through the bush. I'm sure they're moving.'

Peaches said joyously, 'It's him!' and would have stood up to wave in delight, only Harry Carley had the foresight to pull her down.

It was Alec McCrae.

He came out of the bushes, followed by Japanese Charlie and Joe Gunter; right behind was Nona McCrae, and no one was stopping to give her a hand. Even from that distance, they could feel the panic in McCrae's party. They were in a flat spin because suddenly they found themselves without food and water.

Harry Carley said, 'Get down, all of you, quickly. I'm sure that ape's getting suspicious of this island.'

But no one ducked. All wanted to see the next move in the drama. Jay was whispering to no one in particular, 'It must have taken Pat longer than he thought to dig up the water. Or maybe he can't find where he buried the damn stuff.'

And then Peaches blurted out what they were all thinking, 'What happens if Pat comes out on to the beach now, not realising that McCrae's there? He won't stand a chance. He won't stand a chance!' Peaches started to cry. All this was getting her feather-brain down.

Glamour had to cheer her up by

saying, 'They're right opposite where he entered the bush.' So Jay said, rudely, 'Oh, shut up, Glamour! Pat's a wily boy.'

But no one felt happy. They all stood with their hearts in their mouths, expecting to see Rorke come sallying out from the bush, right into the arms of the enemy . . .

McCrae pointed a few times across at the island. Faintly they heard the murmur of voices. For a while; it seemed that poor Nona McCrae was having to stand the fire of their questions; and then suddenly McCrae started diagonally up the beach, his shadow squat and moving before him.

The others followed him into the bush.

Pat Rorke stepped calmly from the screen of bushes the moment they were out of sight and walked leisurely across into the water. And he seemed in no hurry as he swam across.

Harry Carley helped him ashore, then they clambered into the trench and at once the three women were all over him, two of them almost weeping their relief and joy at seeing him safe, the third enjoying herself with a bathful of tears

— Peaches, this time.

When he understood, Rorke was indignant. He said, 'What, you thought I'd come walking out onto the beach without first taking a squint around? Oh, look, you must think I'm first cousin to a dimwit. I don't see what there was to get excited about.'

And he didn't. He'd spotted McCrae and party on the water's edge, and he'd stood behind a tree and listened to their conversation.

Nona McCrae got the edge of all the men's tongues, including her brother's, for in some way failing to protect their food and water supply. And the men were already suffering from thirst and were getting wild in their temper.

McCrae kept saying: 'I don't know where they can be. We've searched every place thoroughly — every place except that.' And he pointed to the little island in the lagoon. He stood, his face dissolved in heavy suspicion. 'Maybe we should take a trip out to make sure they're not hiding on it,' he growled, and then he turned back to question Nona again.

And Nona could only say: 'I don't know where they went. They staggered off with those containers up towards the far end of the runway.'

Japanese Charlie came piping up at that: 'I've been giving thought to this matter, Alec. I can't see how they could have got those heavy containers across to the island there. Now, I think they've got some hiding place up in the deserted camp. That's the way they were headed, Nona says, and people don't go carrying heavy weights all around the island for nothing.'

McCrae allowed himself to be convinced, though Rorke felt that he didn't share the theory. He suddenly started to trudge heavily through the sand, saying unpleasantly: 'Okay, then, let's follow your hunch, Charlie. But it'd better be a good one, otherwise we're gonna have a hell of a thirst by sundown.'

Rorke told them this, grinning. 'It was touch and go. For once I felt I nearly liked that broadcasting little rat, Charlie. Once they suspect we're here they need only sit, one at each side of the lagoon,

and wait until thirst drives us out. Then . . . '
He didn't need to finish the story. They all
could see McCrae and Japanese Charlie,
if not Joe Gunter, potting at their heads
as they came swimming in to surrender.
McCrae couldn't afford to have prisoners.

McCrae would never take any.

8

Swim in the Night

Neither Rorke nor Jay Key touched any of that third bottle of water — they said they'd already had their fill back on shore, and made the other five divide it between them. But just past the middle of the afternoon, they all shared the last bottleful. Seven into one quart of tepid water doesn't add up to much of a ration. But it kept them going; they managed to pass through the long torment of that day without cracking up. And when the sun began to dip behind the horizon, they knew they had won temporarily.

Just before this, they heard a succession of thudding sounds. They all had guesses, and then a majority vote decided that McCrae had found an axe and they were trying to fell a palm tree so as to get at the life-giving coconuts. Whether he succeeded or not they couldn't tell, because the activity was too far away for them to see what was really happening.

And then the sun sank in the far west sea, and Jay Key swore that it sizzled as it went under the water. But then, that was how they all felt — so hot that the water would boil the moment they stepped into it.

When it was dark, Rorke said: 'We're not going to swim to the beach nearest us, where McCrae keeps promenading. He might be sitting out there right now, hoping to see us come up out of the water. We'll go to the far beach and walk round the lagoon. It's farther — ' He shrugged. ' — but I guess it's safer.'

They all hated the thought of swimming in the dark towards that distant blackness that was the shore silhouetted against the night sky. It was the thought of going into the water and swimming into arms that were cold and long, that clung and pulled you under . . .

All the women hung back, and Jay Key was white and shaking, though game to go. Peaches started to have hysterics at the thought of it. She said she'd rather die on the island than take a chance of meeting up with an awful monster out there in the blackness.

So Rorke put his arms round her and said: 'Peaches, honey, don't you see you'll die if you don't get off the island now? You've got to find courage somehow. We can't leave you alone, and if we stay we're all finished.'

So in the end Peaches walked into the water with them. She made Rorke stay close with her to help her, and she sobbed in terror as she breast-stroked frantically across.

In the dark, that lagoon suddenly became as wide as Sydney Harbour; they had ropes on their arms and weights on their feet, and it seemed to take years for them to swim across.

And yet they made it.

They came out like seals, crawling, gasping, Peaches sobbing. Rorke put his arm round her and helped her to stagger up to the bushes. That swim had been just about too much for her, expecting any second to feel something horrible climb up out of the cool, salty depths and catch hold of a leg . . .

There was no hurry now, and Rorke left them to rest for half an hour while he went off on a lone scouting expedition.

When he came back, he said: 'I can't see any trace of them.' It made him uneasy, but they had to go on. He knew the way now, and led them through the night blackness across the neck and out on to the west shore. They were now on the opposite side of the long, narrow island, with its lagoon between crab-like claws, and Rorke felt tolerably safe.

Half a mile along the white blur that was the beach, with the quiet sea gently lapping only a few yards to their left, he struck inland through a belt of trees and bushes, and they found themselves suddenly walking among the silent rows of guns and trucks and derelict planes. Even that was frightening. It seemed wrong; they felt that this place should have been peopled with soldiers and sentries.

Jay whispered: 'Now, where are we gonna hide? In a hut? They'd find us for sure. In a tank?'

'We'd get roasted alive with this sun. No,' whispered Rorke. 'I've got an idea. The most conspicuous feature of the camp is a water tank on top of a tower of latticed steel girders — you know the sort of thing.'

Jay nodded.

'Well, I think because it sticks out a mile, no one'll think of us hiding out up there. Besides, it's got advantages. We should be able to follow their movements pretty well from that height, and if we're spotted, well, we have the water and food and should be able to stand a siege better than they.'

Jay said gently: 'You've forgotten their tree-felling this afternoon. That puts McCrae still one up on us. He still has drink and food — and guns.'

Rorke wasn't to be depressed. He slapped the little engineer on the back and said: 'But we have food and drink, and we didn't have that a few hours ago. Maybe soon we'll have guns — bigger guns than that bastard, too.' And Jay's spirits rose, because he knew that Rorke was on to something.

135

There was an iron ladder that ran straight up the side of the tower and terminated over the top of the tank. Jay went up first, then came back to say that the tank was nice and dry, the floor seemed sound, and there was a wooden cover which would fortunately act as a shade during the daytime.

Rorke sent the three women up, he himself following close behind Peaches because she was weak and nervous and he was afraid she might lose her grip. When they were safely over the top, he descended again, and the four men went quietly into the bush to get the provisions and water.

Rorke was half an hour before he found the place, and they must have dug half a dozen holes before at last he felt sure, and they dug deeper and found the first of the containers. That was a relief.

They carried them back to the camp, pausing every few yards to make sure that McCrae hadn't come up in the darkness. It was nerve-wracking, so near to safety, yet always with the thought that there's many a slip, as the adage runs . . . They couldn't afford any slips. And getting the containers up to the tank was a job.

Prestowe went first, tugging on the handle, with Rorke climbing and taking the weight on his shoulder. Jay Key and Harry followed with a second container. Then they all went back for the last pair of containers.

And then they sat around inside that tank and drank stale water and thoroughly enjoyed it, and finished off the liquor and soft drinks and ate sandwiches and iced cake that was as dry as the sand outside, and they enjoyed that, too. When they'd finished there wasn't much more than a meal each left in the food line, and the water had gone down alarmingly. But Rorke wasn't too bothered. So far they had survived. He had a feeling now that they were beginning to turn the tables on McCrae. Tomorrow could look after itself.

They slept. If the floor was steel and cold, no one seemed to notice it. They were whacked, out to the wide. And yet content.

They felt it next morning, however,

when they awoke with the dawn. They had grown stiff during the night, and they could hardly move at first. Rorke doled out half the food, giving most to the women, and rationed all to half a pint of water each. He calculated that they might have about two days' supply left only, and he wasn't sure about that. You needed an awful lot of water in that torrid climate.

He didn't let anyone move out of the tank until he knew what McCrae and party were doing. He peered cautiously over the edge, making sure that the wooden cover was wedged up behind him, so that the shape of his head didn't show against the skyline.

About half an hour later, he caught his first glimpse of McCrae. He saw him come out on to the beach opposite the little island in the lagoon and stand there and stare across at it for a while. Plainly he was still highly suspicious of the place — and the thought made Rorke grin. McCrae had developed his suspicions just a little late in the day to be of use to him.

McCrae's next actions confirmed that he now suspected the party to be hiding out there in the lagoon, for he sent Japanese Charlie round to the far beach to keep watch from that side. From his lofty position, above even the tallest palm trees on the island, Rorke could just make out the little renegade squatting in the shade, patiently waiting.

Nona was left on the beach at this side, evidently detailed as lookout, while Joe Gunter and big McCrae came inland a hundred yards and began to chop at a palm tree that was leaning at an angle and so would accelerate any attempt to cut through it.

Rorke had to watch carefully, spotting when the cool morning breeze from the sea stirred the intervening palms and let him see the two men working in their midst.

When he felt sure of things, he turned and said: 'McCrae's got Japanese Charlie and Nona keeping watch on the island. He and Duodenal Joe are trying to cut down a tree — probably the one they started cutting last night. I think they'll keep at it till they've succeeded. And that gives us a chance.' He turned to Josie. 'Jo, you take first turn. You stay up here and keep watch. Call out the moment you see any suspicious move on the part of any of them, understand? Peaches'll be stationed right at the foot of the ladder — shout just loud enough for her to hear. And Esther can stand out a bit, so as to relay the call. If there's an alarm, everyone must belt like hell up into this tank.'

Josie said: 'Won't they see us climbing the ladder?'

Rorke said: 'I doubt it. There are plenty of trees in between.' He started to go over the top, and grinned at Josie. 'Don't worry, honey, I'll see you're relieved.'

Then he went quickly down and the others followed. Peaches seemed well able to take care of herself this morning. There were no octopuses up in those trees.

It was a delight to be able to walk about on solid earth again, and for the moment the sun wasn't too hot and they still felt the satisfaction of their breakfast. But the men had work to do.

Harry Carley was the key man now. His job was to find parts within the dump that would build into a transmitter so that they could send out a call for help. He was dubious before he began.

He kept saying: 'You've got to have power for a transmitter, Pat; it isn't as easy as all that to build one.'

Jay said there were lots of car accumulators around the joint; some of them wouldn't be too far gone, and he was pretty sure he could get acid and make distilled water. Rorke thought of the betraying fire that that process would involve, but said nothing until Harry expostulated: 'Yes, but goddam it, Jay, you'll still need to charge your batteries.'

Then Rorke pointed and said: 'I'm not cracked, Harry. Before I started thinking of a transmitter, I'd seen that. Take a look at it and tell me what it looks like.'

'That' was something half-hidden under a tarpaulin.

Harry got excited and said: 'A cycle generator! If I can get that into action, we can start our own broadcasting station. Boy, is that a find!'

Everybody got excited, even Peaches and Esther; Rorke said: 'Harry, you'll make it work, I know you will. And then the fittest member of the party will sit and pedal for a few hours, and the next thing we'll have planes and United States destroyers and God knows what hanging around.'

Esther straightened. 'You can quit thinking of me as the fittest member of the party,' she snapped. 'After last night, I'll never be fit again.'

Then she saw the look in Rorke's eye and knew he was kidding her, but all the same she just stalked away. She didn't unbend easily, the international tennis star, not even here on a Pacific island.

Harry got down to it inside the first hut, not far from the water tower, and Jay acted as forager for him, seeking tools and material. He found unsuspected treasures on his searches, and kept coming back to report to Rorke. He even found a dump of high-octane aviation spirit.

Rorke and Prestowe were busy 'feathering the nest,' as Josie described the operation. They pulled some pretty good spring beds into the tank at the end of a long wire, sufficient for all of them, and then hoisted up bundles of dried grass inside some canvas car covers. The grass, sandwiched between two layers of canvas, made quite effective mattresses.

All during this time, one of the women kept watch from the top of the tower, with another woman stationed at the foot, and the third acting as a relay for messages halfway across to where the men were working.

Once they had an alarm. It was about two hours after they'd started work. They were all keyed up, senses alert for danger, so that when Peaches called and the cry was relayed, everyone ran like mad for the tower. Glamour girl went up the ladder so fast she would have passed Josie if the rungs had been nine inches wider.

And when they all came perspiring over the top, Peaches only got indignant and said: 'What came over you? I just called to tell you they'd got the tree down.'

Rorke sighed and wiped his dripping face with his bare arm and said: 'Honey, I'm sure somewhere someone loves you.' And little Jay Key echoed their thoughts with a short 'Somewhere!'

They had a rest before returning, and

looked out over the island towards the distant blue lagoon. Peaches prattled on: 'They've been splitting coconuts with their axe or whatever it is. I saw them while you were coming like a lot of scared rabbits up the ladder.' Her sarcasm was wasted.

They saw Joe and McCrae go down to the beach where Nona sat, their arms loaded with coconuts. Joe split some of them and Nona started drinking, and the way she went at those coconuts they could see she was pretty frantic with thirst. They knew what it felt like.

Then Joe Gunter went round the beach with his load of coconuts and the machete (that was what the men thought it to be), and little Japanese Charlie saw him coming and came galloping round halfway to meet him. Then there was more coconut splitting. It made them wistful, up there in that hot, dried-out water tank, to see the lavish quantities of cool, fresh coconut milk being absorbed in such large quantities.

Rorke sighed and said: 'Just as soon as we get guns, we'll chop a tree down, then we'll bathe in the damn stuff.'

Harry hoisted his heavy thighs on to the edge of the tank and said: 'You tell me where we can get guns on this island without stunning McCrae or partners first. I haven't seen any small-arms.'

They descended. When they got to the bottom, Harry spilt the news that this was going to be a long job. It might be days before he could get a transmitter working.

'Days?' Rorke stood and doodled with the shadow of his left foot. 'You know we can't last out so long. We'll be off our heads with thirst, even if that murdering swine doesn't tumble to our hideout first.'

The four men looked at each other. They had started the morning too optimistically; now they saw again their truly desperate plight. After a moment, Harry shrugged and started to move away, saying: 'Well, I might just as well get working as fast as I can. Maybe you'll think of something, Pat.'

Rorke walked away, down among the trunks. The dormant idea that had lain back of his brain for the last few hours stirred and woke and suddenly became very active. From the top of the tower, Peaches saw him go nosing from one vehicle to another, and then suddenly he came running back and grabbed Jay, and the two went flying together up among the vehicles.

Peaches knew they were on to something, and it was tantalising to have to keep watch on McCrae and party when she wanted to see what the pair were doing.

They had a break at mid-day, and all climbed slowly, tiredly back into the tank. It was pleasanter up there now — there was green stuff all over the floor to make the place cool, and Prestowe had cleverly tilted the cover in the direction of the prevailing wind so that the breeze fanned down on to them. And the wooden cover gave them shade.

Suddenly, all at once, optimism came surging back as they found the party spirit that had been there at breakfast. It was due, Rorke knew, to the exhilaration of being here in the clear sky, high enough to look out over the green island to the blue sea stretching to the horizon in all directions. They could even see the nearest of the other Tahao islands, about twelve miles northwest of them.

For the first time, they found comfort in their situation. The tank now seemed cooler than anywhere else on the island, shaded and breezy, and their beds were delightfully comfortable.

They drank their ration of water, then polished off all that was left of the food. And then Peaches said: 'Pat, you're up to something. Tell us — go on!'

Rorke rolled on to his side on his bed and looked at Jay. The little bald-headed airplane engineer smiled and nodded, so Rorke said: 'We didn't intend to tell you until we were completely sure, but — well, we think we stand a chance now.'

'A chance?' Everyone echoed his words. Esther stopped trying to comb her matted hair with her fingers and said quickly: 'You've found some old rifles?'

'Not quite as good as that. But Jay and I have found a tank that we think can be made to move, and that tank's got a mighty useful gun up in its turret that I know I can fire.'

147

They were all on their feet in a moment. They couldn't believe their ears. 'It's fantastic!' whispered Josie, but the way she said it, she didn't seem to want to make it sound impossible.

Rorke said drily: 'Sitting up in this blamed nest is a bit fantastic, too, but — here we are.'

Josie came over and sat on his bed, and then Peaches and Glamour came and sat along with her. Glamour said: 'I'll kill you if it's another of your gags,' but Rorke was sincere.

'Ask Jay, then. It's so damned crazy that I couldn't take to the idea myself at first, but — well, I just couldn't get away from those rows of tanks right under my nose, so I went around and found they weren't quite as derelict as all the rust makes 'em appear. In fact, those tanks are in better condition than the trucks or airplanes — there's less in them to rot, I suppose. Jay's been and had a look at one of them, and he's confident that he can cannibalise parts from other tanks and have this one going in a matter of a day.'

'And the gun you talked about?'

Peaches said, breathless with excitement.

'I can clean it. And there's ammunition. I don't trust the HE, but the armour-piercing should be enough for McCrae and friends.'

Harry Carley stopped wiping his thick forearm with a piece of canvas and grinned. 'You ever fired a gun or driven a tank?'

Jay gave him the answer: 'Look, Harry, if I don't find a way of driving that tank in some sort of fashion, you can hand me on a plate to Bogyman McCrae.'

Rorke said comfortably: 'And I'll learn how to make a noise with that gun, you bet your life I will.' Then he told them that Jay had found an amphibian that was in surprisingly good condition, and if they could patch the hull they might be able to get away from the island.

Peaches nearly had hysterics at the thought. 'Oh, Pat!' she said. 'How wonderful! What would we have done without you both? I could kiss you for that!'

Rorke grabbed her quick, saying: 'Don't change your mind, honey. I won't scream or do anything!'

Next moment the three women were

on to him — and was he enjoying it! And Glamour seemed to enjoy it, too, that scramble.

But it was hot, even pretending to wrestle, and they soon stopped and went back to their improvised mattresses. Rorke sighed his content and turned luxuriously over on to his side for half an hour's rest before resuming work, pleased — exhilarated by the idea that held such promise of salvation for them.

And yet at the back of his brain a note had started sounding that something was wrong. Something was wrong up here in the nest.

9

The Problem Child

The feeling persisted. Somewhere inside his brain was a record of some little thing that he had noted that wasn't right, but he couldn't remember what was on the record. He kept moving uneasily, his happiness steadily evaporating. Finally he got up in a bad temper and peered cautiously out over the island.

In the far distance he could see Joe Gunter and Japanese Charlie in the shade of a clump of coconut palms, while closer, on this side of the lagoon, were the McCraes. He caught his breath suddenly. No, that was Nona McCrae only, lying there. Big Alec McCrae, Hate No. 1 to the American nation, wasn't with her.

It made him uneasy, and yet his subconscious mind was saying: *That's not it — it's something else you should worry about*; but he couldn't figure out what it was.

Until he saw the bed right by the curving iron ladder that came in over the edge of the tank.

It was Prestowe's bed. And it was empty.

Rorke's voice startled them, bringing them out of their doze. 'Where's Prestowe gone?'

They came swinging up into sitting position at that, all of them, nerves tautened, knowing instinctively that some action had been precipitated that had put them all in peril again.

No one spoke for a second, and then everyone talked. Pat Rorke stood over them and put the pieces together. Prestowe had been there, some of them remembered, even while he was telling them about the tank and the gun. Josie argued: 'But he couldn't have climbed out when we were all down on our beds, because one of us would have seen him for certain.'

No one bothered to say anything after that. All knew when John Prestowe had gone — and why.

He must have slipped away during the

commotion when the women were making a fuss about Rorke . . . because of it.

Rorke rubbed his fingers through his hair wearily, and thought: *Oh, God, what it is to have a problem child in the party — mummy's boy!*

It was that complex of Prestowe's, the product of all his mother-inspired frustrations and repressions. Wanting to be like any normal young man and enjoy the company of women, yet denying himself these pleasures — and being unable to stand by and see other normal, balanced men have them. Seeing the women larking around Rorke must have driven him out of the nest.

But where? Rorke sat up stiffly. McCrae was on the prowl. McCrae couldn't rest like the others. McCrae was somewhere in the bush, and maybe he'd come across that obstinate young fool.

Rorke jumped across to the edge of the tank again and peered over, dread in his heart — fear, not that McCrae would kill Prestowe, but that he wouldn't kill him. Because if he captured him alive, he might get the secret from him of their hiding place, and then they would be sunk, and he didn't feel that Prestowe would hold out much if McCrae got to work with his scientific torture . . . the tricks he had taught the Japanese to use on captured Americans.

And back of his mind was another, even more horrible, thought. That in his insane jealousy, Prestowe might have gone to McCrae deliberately to betray them. When you got a fellow as balled up inside as Prestowe, you never knew where you stood.

Rorke couldn't see McCrae. But he saw that Nona McCrae had disappeared from her position on the beach. And Japanese Charlie and Joe Gunter were running round the lagoon from the far side.

Rorke turned. The others were waiting, and he knew they were dreading what he might have to say to them. He was thinking furiously, so that for a moment they had to sit and watch and wait. Then he swallowed.

'Look, I think McCrae's caught hold of Prestowe.'

Peaches said: 'Well, he shouldn't have

gone out on his own. You said for us not to.'

Rorke said slowly: 'Yes, but there's more to it than that, Peaches. You see, I think McCrae's got Prestowe alive, and it would be better if the fellow were dead.'

Josie sucked in her breath quickly. 'You mean, he'll — hurt Prestowe?'

Rorke shrugged. 'What do you think? Why does all America hate him so much? Because he tortured captured Americans so as to make them betray their own country. He's expert at such work, none more so.'

So Josie asked, bewildered: 'But why should he torture him?'

The other two men suddenly rose. They understood now. Rorke said: 'To try to find out where we're hiding.' He turned to Harry Carley. 'Why had the fellow to do it today? Tomorrow we'd have had the gun ready and could have held them off. Now . . . ' He looked at his bare hands expressively. He went on after a pause. 'But we're not licked yet. Look, Harry, we're done if McCrae manages to trap us all up this tower. He can sit below and wait until thirst licks us. But it's still the safest place on the island for the women. They've got to stay here, and you, Harry, must stay with them. Gun or no gun, you can hold out against McCrae if you keep your eye on top of that ladder.'

He and Jay moved between the beds towards the way out. Josie whispered, 'Oh, Pat, just when we felt on top of the world. And what are you going to do?'

Rorke said viciously: 'Keep fightin' back at that snake!' He peered over cautiously, then swung himself astride the tank. 'Goodbye, don't worry,' he said with a smile. 'Jay and I will be fighting back down below, and maybe we'll find a way of turning the tables on him.'

They went down the ladder as fast as they dared, and when they reached the bottom Rorke said, 'We must split up, Jay. Look, you go and get working on that tank engine. That tank's as good a hiding place as any for the moment. And time's precious.'

'And you?'

'I'm going to see if I can get Prestowe out of their hands before he cracks.'

'You think he'll crack?'

'With McCrae operating, I'm sure he will.'

They parted. Rorke cut across to the lagoon and then came quickly down the beach. He knew he was taking a risk, moving so fast without heed of cover, but he had a hunch that right now McCrae would be very occupied.

Part way along the beach was a miniature bay, perhaps twenty yards across. It was so shallow that Rorke went straight into it.

He was almost across when big McCrae started to come down the beach. He had his gun in his hand. The light glinted on his rimless glasses, and there was the faintest suspicion of a smile on his face.

McCrae was just a shade too confident, and Rorke's reaction was so swift that it took the renegade by surprise. Rorke was running, coming out in the sandy shallows. He didn't check his pace as he should have done when he saw that gun; instead he kicked, like any kid at the seaside, and a spray of water fanned up towards the advancing gunman.

It doesn't matter who you are, what you are; when you see water hurtling towards you, involuntarily you flinch and draw away.

That's what McCrae did. He ducked. It spoilt his aim. And some of the sand and water smeared his spectacles so that his vision was distorted.

Up in the tower they had seen it all happen. Seen Rorke sprinting along, seen McCrae step out of the bush, gun levelled. Peaches screamed, Esther shouted with horror, and Josie moaned and turned so that she couldn't see the end . . .

They heard a shot — they couldn't see the water spray up from that distance, and it mystified them just then — but Rorke didn't go down. Instead he went in a long sprawling dive that ended with his head ramming into McCrae, sending him toppling into the sand.

Rorke rolled across the body and grabbed the automatic and tried to tear it from McCrae's grasp. But McCrae was strong with his weight, and he held on for dear life, shouting hoarsely, 'Charlie — Joe!'

Then he pulled the trigger again, and

the concussion of the explosion travelled in a swift jar up Rorke's arm; he felt his hand blister, and was amazed to find that he hadn't lost a finger. But he let go. Next time the bullet might go through his hand, and he needed it.

Something sang over his head, to be followed quickly by the sharp crack of a more distant automatic. He looked up, coming to his feet. Japanese Charlie and Joe Gunter had come out of the bushes farther alone the beach. Charlie was walking calmly, unhurried, his glasses reflecting whitely as the sun bounced up from the hot yellow beach, taking pot shots as if Rorke were a rabbit.

Rorke started to go for cover. Before he left McCrae, however, he stamped on the hand so that the automatic got filthed up with sand. McCrae shouted with pain and rolled like a landed turtle on to his back. Rorke went headlong into the bushes, just as another bullet smacked through the air behind his head. Japanese Charlie wasn't such a good marksman as McCrae. Rorke passed out of sight of the tower at that.

He didn't have any idea in mind, but

just went plunging into the bush. This way would bring him out somewhere along the old runway, he knew, and that was as good a place as any.

He found himself following the trail broken by McCrae when he came down to the beach. He was running hell for leather along it when he heard a pistol shot just ahead. He stood on his heels and came to a violent stop. He couldn't understand it. He'd seen McCrae, Charlie and Joe Gunter, and they'd had the three guns on the island. Now he was hearing another pistol, and that was ahead of him.

It made him reckless and he went forward, not too carefully either. He came out into a clearing that was shaded by palms and with a window in the bushes that gave a lovely view across the beach and foaming surf out to the broad blue Pacific Ocean beyond.

But he wasn't interested in the scenery. Something was moving in the bushes at the edge of the clearing. Then he caught a glimpse of pants legs and knew it to be Prestowe. He went across and parted the tall grasses and looked down. Then his knees went weak and slowly he knelt beside the man.

Prestowe was going from the world, rapidly. There was no colour in his face, and it was curiously small-looking, the eyes turned upwards under faintly flickering lids. He seemed to stir and sigh, and that was the last sound on earth of John Prestowe, a lonely old widow's boy, far away in Australia.

And Rorke was left looking at that naked body, at the things that had been done to it. He was drenched with the horror of what he saw, and he couldn't take his eyes away from it. The things they had done to this boy . . .

Nona McCrae said, tiredly, 'I wasn't supposed to, but I shot him. I couldn't stand it, the way he lay and moaned. I put him out of his misery, like a dog.'

Rorke lifted his head slowly. There was a mist of grief clouding his eyes. He saw that Nona was standing across in the clearing now. She looked almost as dead as Prestowe.

He said, 'My God, the things they did to him!'

But she shook her head. 'Not they — *him*. My husband. *Mine*. He did it, every bit of it, and he made us watch. He took Joe's gun away after a time because the way Joe was it looked as though he might have killed Alec himself. Alec did all this to him, while Charlie argued that he was justified in doing what he was doing. Charlie can always find a reason for whatever he wants to do.'

Rorke was looking at the automatic in her hand, watching it, fascinated. If only he could get hold of it, he'd feel almost on level terms with the gunmen. He rose and came back through the lush grasses. He came slowly, casually, because he didn't want to alarm her. He said, 'Didn't Prestowe talk, then?'

'Him? No. He passed out without saying anything. Just looked pale and obstinate. It made Alec mad and he went too hard and the boy fainted. Then Alec went to have a look at that island in the lagoon, because he still thinks some of your party are on it. There's some branches over there going dead, he says . . .'

Rorke came forward quickly to get the gun. Nona went back and levelled it. Her eyes were dead, her voice lifeless, but her words held him back. 'Don't try to get this gun, please. I'll have to shoot you if you do. I don't like hurting anyone, but I'd have to do it. You see, you don't know what Alec would do to me if I let you get away with this gun. He's done things to me before, awful things. That's why he gave me Joe's gun — he knows I daren't let him down, ever.'

Rorke knew that he'd never get the gun now. He knew she would shoot, and getting shot wasn't going to help the party. There were only six left now; better not make it five. God knew, the way things were they'd soon be down to that number.

He heard heavy bodies trampling through the bush towards him. He said, 'Why don't you shoot him, your husband? That's quite an idea, you know.'

She watched him with eyes as dull as old rags, then shook her head. 'I can't. Someday I might have the courage, but he's left me none now, not even enough to shoot him when he isn't looking. He deserves it, I know.' And then she said, 'Go quickly; they're coming. I couldn't stand having to watch all that torture again. I'll tell them I had to shoot Prestowe when you came through and tried to get away with him. Yes, that's what I'll tell him. It's quite a good idea, and I'll get out of trouble that way.' Rorke, watching her, saw that she was going childish in her mind. It wouldn't take much more to shove her right over the edge. He felt sorry for her.

McCrae's grey bulk could be discerned among the trees now, so Rorke nodded to Nona and slipped quietly away into the bushes.

Deliberately after that he circled the clearing, coming within sight of McCrae, who shouted and loosened off a shot that was miles wide at that distance.

They saw the next bit of the drama from up on top of the tower. Rorke came racing like fury out of the bushes and down the beach into the lagoon. He was taking a chance on this move — swimming isn't a quick way of covering distance, especially if you're out of breath to start with. But he risked it.

He drew the trio on to the beach after him, and he was out of range when they came to the water's edge and started to fire. When he crawled out on to the island, he knew he was quite safe, and McCrae didn't even bother to try for range.

Rorke rested against the sand wall that Prestowe had so carefully built, in full view of the gunmen on the beach. They couldn't understand what he was doing up in the tower; but Rorke was playing for time — time for Jay Key to get that engine into working order.

His ruse worked. For half an hour, the three men sat and talked on the beach, as if in argument. Finally McCrae seemed to give an order, for Japanese Charlie started the long walk round the lagoon to his old position on the far side.

Rorke took his time, even then. He gave Charlie a few minutes' start, and then stood up and talked loudly at no one. But to McCrae on the beach it looked as though he was speaking to someone within that wall of sand that had the growth of wilting vegetation. What McCrae couldn't understand was why no one showed up, now that their hiding place was plainly discovered.

Then Rorke climbed over the wall and disappeared from sight. From the tower — but not from the beach — they saw him sneak out the far way and swim quickly across to the distant shore and then climb out and go quickly across the beach and into the thick vegetation beyond. Twenty minutes later, Charlie was round there, keeping watch on an empty island.

Then they heard Rorke start to climb the ladder, and behind him was Jay Key. He came over the top, pretty well exhausted, but pleased. The women and Harry came crowding round, delighted to see him.

Rorke said, 'After that, I could do with a drink — and so could Jay, I guess.' He stretched out on his bed. He was nearly dry already. He just said, 'McCrae doesn't know we're here.'

Harry asked quietly, 'Prestowe?'

'Dead.'

The news shocked the women and they all sat in silence. Rorke knew it was up to him to snap them out of the mood; they'd never get anywhere, sorrowing. He swung his tired limbs off the bed and stretched. He doled out the water and then went across, and looked out over the lagoon.

Charlie was in the shade right across from the tiny island, and movements on the near shore indicated that McCrae and Joe Gunter were keeping watch from this side. Rorke didn't move until he knew for certain that both men were there, but then he turned and smiled and said, 'I've got the gang watching a deserted island. They think we're trapped out there and they're sitting back in the hope that thirst will drive us into surrender.'

News like that cheered them. He pressed it home. 'Jay says a few more hours' work and we'll have a tank chasin' 'em through the scrub. Won't that be a change, huh?'

They went back to their old positions, the women keeping watch and acting as relays for warning messages, while Harry got back to making the generator work and Jay Key and Rorke went inside the tank.

Just before dusk, McCrae went for a wander into the bush, but it was only to get some coconuts from the fallen palm. He went back to the beach, and then Joe Gunter went round to Charlie with supplies. Josie had given the alarm when McCrae moved, so they were all up top, watching. Rorke said, 'McCrae intends to sit up all night by the look of things. Well, that gives us another hour of work, Jay. Let's get moving.' And Harry borrowed Glamour to do some steady pedaling for him.

Daylight was precious; they used it, working right until the last gleam faded from the sky. And then they went back to the nest — all except Rorke, who said something vague about trying to get something and went off into the darkness. It worried them, and they sat above and listened for sounds of his return. Then they heard the low, musical note as someone started to climb up the vibrating steel ladder.

Harry stood by, as he always did, with a stick. But it was Rorke who came sliding over the top, Rorke with a canvas full of coconuts. He had been and raided McCrae's private supply.

They slept well that night, far better that the three watchers round the lagoon. They had beds, tolerably soft mattresses, and they'd had coconut milk for supper as well as plenty of coconut to chew. It felt like a feast to them . . .

10

Rorke Opens Fire

McCrae wasn't a fool. He tumbled to it early next morning that the island was deserted. How he came to the conclusion, Rorke and party never knew, but from his actions it became unmistakable. An hour or two after sunrise, they saw McCrae swim boldly out to the island and walk over it. The way he did it, they knew he was just confirming a suspicion.

He swam back. Josie sent the news down the ladder. Harry was sweating grimly in his stifling hut; more, sweat, skin and bad language were being lost inside a tank that was like a kitchen oven on baking day.

Harry Carley was perturbed when he heard the news and he came hurriedly across and talked to them in the tank. Inside he could tell by the gasps and grunting that the two men were working all out. He called softly, 'Pat?'

They stopped working, and Rorke shoved his head out up top. He was fried raw red from the heat inside, and the sweat ran in an oily stream over his face and down his naked, muscular chest. Harry thought, *The way he's losing moisture, he'll need a lot of drink to keep him going.*

He said, 'How are things, Pat . . . ? I'm worried. They'll be combing the island for us again, and they've still got the guns, don't forget.'

Rorke swung his legs over the edge and sat and thought. He was tired from the previous day's exertions and a bit depressed. 'If only we could keep them quiet for another three or four hours.'

They heard Josie call down the ladder at that moment. Rorke forgot his tiredness; he had a hunch what this meant. He said, 'We can't move this damned can, not until Jay puts all the bits together.'

'But it will go — then?'

Rorke nodded. 'I'm sure of it. Jay's made a good job of the engine . . . ' He looked at Harry. 'How are you coming on?' The belle of Wimbledon was streaking so fast towards them that her light summer dress was up round her waist — not that she gave a hang.

Harry Carley said, 'It's a lousy job. If I get on the air tomorrow, I'll think I've done wonders.'

Rorke sighed. 'You'd just have to keep going, Harry, that's all. So will Jay. Here's Glamour coming to tell us that McCrae's on the prowl again.'

'And you?'

I'm going to try to hold McCrae back for a few hours.' He patted the tank. 'I've already got some rounds of ammunition inside, and I can traverse the gun through any arc. It's like trying to hit a mosquito with a pea-shooter. I've got to use armour-piercing stuff because HE would blow up in the barrel, I'm certain; the stuff's been lying exposed too long.'

Esther came hurtling up and fell into Rorke's arms. Harry said, 'Why do they all come to you, Pat? Why don't they come to me sometime?'

Rorke said soothingly, 'Don't tell me, Esther. I know. There's a line of 'em across the island and they're beating down from the lagoon towards us. Right?'

Still gasping for breath, Esther nodded. Then she started to pull him towards the tower. But Rorke shook his head. 'You and the women get back up there, and don't show yourself. But we're staying on working. I've got a gun going; I'm hoping to hold 'em off long enough for Jay to fix the engine; and then we'll chase 'em round and round the island while Harry gets an SOS tapped out.'

One thing about Esther Van Kass, she didn't waste time in arguing — not when the safety of Esther Van Kass was at stake. She nodded understanding, wheeled and skimmed back like a lovely fleeting swallow. They saw her say something to Peaches, then skip round her and go up that tower almost as fast as she had ever made the winner's jump over a tennis net. Peaches was a poor second, but her speed was improving enormously.

Harry went off in a hurry to his quiet hut in the corner. Rorke loaded the gun and then stood up and watched across the neck of the island by the end of the runway. Down below, Jay Key worked in a cloud of steam and lost weight at the rate of an ounce a minute.

And he swore. Softly. Incessantly. Oh, so viciously!

Once he stopped to ask, 'Let me know when you fire that cannon, Pat. If you can fire it.'

Rorke said, 'I'll lay an even ten bucks I learn in the next few minutes.'

Jay Key said mechanically, 'I'll take you.'

Rorke's eyes narrowed at that second, and he started to traverse the turret. Very softly he called down, 'Take a hold of your pants, Jay. The battle's opening up!'

Someone was moving through the bushes at the end of the runway, about a couple of hundred yards away. It was at the end of Main Street, as they'd called the central avenue between the lines of sagging, weather-bleached wood huts. Rorke thought, *Take a walk down Main Street, bud, and see what comes to you!* He was squinting along the sights, thinking, *If only McCrae steps out of cover!* He was gripping the gun so hard that his body was trembling with the nervous tension of the moment.

Then someone stepped cautiously out on to the end of the street, just around the corner of the farthermost hut. Only it wasn't big city man McCrae — it was Renegade Charlie. He was coming slowly down the street, looking into the huts. Rorke would have liked to have waited until he was at the end of his gun barrel and then opened fire, but he could hear other movements in the bush west of the graveyard, so he let go without further waiting.

Inside that tank, the noise was so devastating to their unpractised ears that it threw them into a daze. There was a reek of cordite fumes, a blast of heat, a rush of displaced air.

One moment little Charlie was coming blinking behind his glasses, gun in hand, but not really afraid. The next second something screamed within inches of him, hit the blue sea beyond and ricocheted in a long, whining hop before plunging deep into the ocean.

Charlie didn't remember falling, but when he found his senses he was lying on his back, the sun blinding down into his face. From the top of the tower, three enthralled women who weren't supposed to be looking saw him suddenly pick himself up and fly out of sight around a corner. Japanese Charlie had had the fright of his life that morning.

Rorke got his wits back, sneezing as the cordite bit up his nose. He swung the turret, loading clumsily, fumblingly. He was stone deaf for the moment, but he thought he saw a movement in the trees back beyond the last line of trucks, and he sighted quickly and fired again.

Again that deafening, shattering weight of sound on their eardrums, the tank reverberating, persisting with diminishing echoes. That cordite smell . . . and the blast of heat.

Five feet up, a palm tree suddenly jumped back a couple of feet, its leafy top agitating hysterically. Then it dropped and then inclined in one long accelerating fall that filled the air with the noise of its destructive end among the close-packed bushes below.

Dust blew about, then settled. Rorke

loaded and peered anxiously out. He didn't know if he had done any damage, apart from felling an inoffensive coconut palm.

He watched from the turret for the next hour, Jay Key swearing and working below; then Josie suddenly appeared. Rorke said sharply, 'Josie, get back — at once!'

Josie clambered up the tread of the tank. She had the water container with her. She smiled and said, 'It's all right, Pat. They're all up at the far end of the runway, trying to get their nerve back, I guess. I thought you'd be thirsty.'

It was all the water they had. Josie said the women would manage on coconuts, but Rorke wasn't to be kidded. He knew they hadn't any. So he raced to the fallen palm and came back with as many as he could carry to the foot of the tower. It meant several journeys up for the women, but while the gunmen were down the island that wouldn't matter. Then he went along to the tank lines, where Josie was waiting with a subdued, non-swearing Jay Key.

Jay came panting up for air when he heard Rorke. He was in a filthy state and getting desperate with the heat. He wiped his face with his arm and said, 'Oh, God, Pat, can't you come down and help me with some of this lifting? It's murder, I tell you. I could finish in an hour or so, if you'd give me a hand now.'

Rorke said, 'Look, Josie, you get the women to take those coconuts up top, but you keep watch while I help Jay. The moment you see any movement from the McCrae bunch, yell your head off, only keep under cover so they won't know where you are.'

Josie nodded and ran off. Rorke and Jay Key finished off the water between them and then got to work. It was exasperatingly difficult because they hadn't all the tools they required, and that meant improvisation, often with doubtful results. But still — they were coming along . . .

Fifteen minutes or so later, Josie shouted to them. Rorke swung himself up, waved to Josie, and then settled behind his gun.

Half an hour passed. There was a deathly silence over the island, and it wasn't reassuring. Rorke knew what it meant — the trio were creeping up on them, trying to find out the meaning of this big gun they now possessed, to see how dangerous it was.

Below, Jay suddenly said, 'Keep 'em off just a little longer, Pat. Just another half an hour and we'll chase those devils up hill and down dale.'

Watching, Rorke said, 'There are no hills on this island, Jay — but we'll chase 'em, just the same.'

Then something spanged on the turret in front of him, almost immediately followed by the sharp crack of an automatic. Rorke dropped under cover and traversed. For a second he had caught a movement back of the end hut, not too far from where Harry Carley was working. They mustn't get nearer, mustn't capture Harry . . .

He didn't wait to see his target again; he put an armour-piercing shell smack through both walls of the flimsy hut. The hut promptly collapsed at one end; now more expertly loading, Rorke saw two or three raising a dense cloud of yellow dust. Frantically, figures scurried quickly away into the bush.

'Round two to us,' he called down to

Jay. 'Let's hope that keeps 'em quiet for another hour or so and then you'll have finished.'

But five minutes later, the McCrae bunch were back to the attack again. McCrae didn't lose his head because of a big noise, and by now he'd figured out the situation — they had a gun, but it was too big for them to move.

This time McCrae showed greater tenacity. Rorke saw him as he crossed the open ground between the bushes and the west end of the runway. Hopefully he banged off a shot that shook the nuts from a distant palm but didn't fell it. Then McCrae called, and the other pair skipped hurriedly across to where he was hiding behind the end truck of a line of three-tonners.

Rorke could see the top of the truck, but that was all; the other lines of vehicles and guns overlapped in his sight, so that he couldn't send a shell down to where they lay on the ground behind the three-tonner.

His face was strained now, knowing what this meant. These lines of vehicles gave excellent cover to the gunmen; if they were careful they could come so close that he couldn't depress the gun sufficiently to hit them. After that they could stand upright and walk up to the tank and shoot him and Jay out of hand — there were plenty of holes in this tank that hadn't been made by the designer.

He called, 'How long now, Jay?'

Jay's voice, frantic, came floating up. 'I don't know, Pat. Maybe a quarter of an hour, maybe much more.'

So Pat Rorke said, 'If you don't get her moving within five minutes, you'll never have a chance to practise on another tank engine.'

What little Jay Key said at that, blisteringly, suggested that after this he didn't want to see another tank engine as long as he lived.

Rorke saw a movement partway along the three-tonners; he got the gun round, sighted, and fired. The three-tonner seemed to jump into the air and lose half its sheeting in rust, but otherwise nothing else happened. Rorke could only hope that it would make the trio cautious and keep them moving slowly. Time, time! They had to play for time! Minutes — seconds even — were vital now.

He was thinking, 'So near, yet so far. We're almost there, almost at the point of turning the tables on these murdering sons of so-and-sos.' Almost there . . . but not quite.

Rorke saw the grey of McCrae's suit. It was up by the second line of trucks. He belted off another round and knocked a cabin forward on to the bonnet.

Then McCrae showed up for a second in the third line, by the amphibians. Rorke got a round away that put an end to that vehicle ever floating again. He hoped it wasn't the one in pretty good condition that Jay had spoken about.

Four more lines of trucks to go, and then the McCrae lot would be among the tanks. They were coming nearer down the lines now, all three of them. Rorke could smell gasoline. He held his fire for a few seconds and then tried to anticipate and blazed off a round that mashed in the front of a jeep that had already taken a battering in a previous battle. But

McCrae and Co. hadn't come along quite so fast and were back of another.

Coming up. Getting bolder. Moving in quick rushes. Through to the last line of trucks. So near that the next few yards would bring them to safety. Then all three rushed the gap across to the tanks. They weren't sixty yards away now. Rorke thought, *What do we have to lose?* and started loading and firing as hard as he could go. There was always the chance that flying metal from the vehicles would do some damage.

He could hardly see now for dust, and he was so deaf that the only noise that registered was when the gun roared under his hand. The tank was vibrating; it was hell, an inferno. And by now, the knowledgeable McCrae would be under the gun and running up.

Rorke tumbled and sat down on the litter of empty shell cases. Something had gone wrong with him. He found he couldn't stand — or else everything was swaying. Sweating and gasping, he pulled himself up behind the gun.

He saw a hut walk steadily towards him

and collapse on top of the tank. Didn't see anything for a second or two, but lived in a world of rending wood that screamed its protests. Then he saw another hut walking steadily towards him and understood.

Jay had got the tank on the move.

11

Peaches Walks into Danger

Rorke stood in the turret and waved and cheered. At the last moment, they had met with success. Now they could chase McCrae.

And then he saw that hut almost on top of them and shouted over the roaring, revving engine, 'What the hell are you doing, Jay? Can't you see that damned hut?'

Jay just looked back at him pityingly. 'One damned tread's sticking and pulling us round in a circle. I haven't figured what to do about it yet. Have you any ideas?'

Rorke thought, 'To hell with the huts, anyway!' They were keeping away from McCrae, the way they were travelling.

The hut collapsed as they marched through it; they lived in a darkened world for a moment and then it pulled away and

185

they found themselves out on Main Street. Jay halted the tank and played around with one tread until they were facing back down towards the graveyard. Rorke caught a glimpse of a startled but delighted face in a hut opposite — Harry Carley's. Then Harry ducked back out of sight.

Rorke saw the massive figure of McCrae over by one of the collapsed huts. He didn't know what to do for the moment, so Rorke gave him a few ideas.

He whipped the gun round, loaded and fired. But McCrae had seen the movement and was off like a suddenly agile elephant. McCrae was big and not far away, but you can't hit such a moving target with a tank gun. Rorke couldn't, anyway.

Rorke stood up top and roared, 'After 'em, Jay! Let's drive the devils into the sea!'

But Jay, wrestling with the controls down below, shouted, 'I'll try, Pat, but the damned left tread keeps sticking.'

The chase started, a fantastic manhunt with a man driving a tank who had never

186

handled a tank before and a man firing a gun who had never seen such a gun until a few hours previously. And the tank kept careering leftwards at intervals, so that their trail was a series or arcs most of the time.

But it must have been frightening to the men back among the vehicles to see that mighty, impregnable (to them) monster bearing down on them, a big gun booming at all too frequent intervals. They ran for it.

Rorke blazed away, but under the circumstances he was never within feet of the target. Rorke got Jay to drive down to the far end of the graveyard and then systematically began to hunt back along the lines. He wanted the McCrae bunch away from this end of the island, penned on the narrow point that formed one jaw around the lagoon.

They paraded along the end of the rows, Rorke spanging steel down when he saw a movement. After a while, the trio retreated voluntarily and finally took to the bushes. Probably Japanese Charlie and Joe Gunter kept on running then, but

187

Rorke saw the bulk of McCrae among the trees and knew he was waiting on the fringe in the hope of getting in a lucky shot.

He shouted down to Jay, 'Get into those trees. Let's finish McCrae once and for all!'

But that sticking tread was getting worse, and Jay couldn't control the tank at times. They lurched into the brush, flattening it, and then hit a tree which they had intended to miss. The tank climbed a bit and then the tree took the cowardly course of lying down.

Jay tried again and set the engines roaring, filling the island with sound, but they only crashed into more trees and brought down a murderous rain of coconuts, so Rorke said, 'Pack it in, Jay. We won't get anywhere like this. Get back into the open.'

From the open, back of the huts, they could mount guard and drive off any attack that developed. Then he saw McCrae back among the trees and he called to Jay to stop so that he could have a steadier aim. Then he settled down, just within the shade of the first palm trees, to blast shot after shot into the vegetation in the general direction of where he had seen McCrae. When he remembered and found himself with only two rounds left, he stopped firing and told Jay to move back close to the water tower. By that time, McCrae had probably got tired and moved well down the island, anyway. Rorke got out quickly and loaded up with ammunition.

Harry came along, and then Josie and Peaches came down from the nest. Josie called, when she was still high up, 'They're all moving down to the lagoon. Esther's keeping watch.'

Then the women grabbed hold of the sweating, smoke-blackened men as they crawled out of the stifling atmosphere of the tank and hugged them.

'We thought they had you,' Josie said. 'We watched it all from above. It was terrible; I've never been through such a nerve-racking ordeal in my life, watching those awful men creeping up on you. They weren't more than twenty yards away when suddenly the tank came crawling out of the line and went ramming into that hut.'

Harry was smashing open some nuts and they all drank. Jay said, 'I'm beginning to hate coconuts already. What I'd give for some food!' But Harry said it wouldn't kill them for another day, and by that time he'd have a radio call-out.

Another day ... With such a tricky customer as McCrae, anything could happen before that vital message took the air. They'd improved their position a lot in the last few minutes, but not as much as he had hoped when he'd first realised that Jay had got the tank to move. Still, keeping alive so long was one mighty fine achievement.

Rorke said, 'We don't need to worry about coconuts now. Little Daisy here must have knocked a couple of thousand down to the ground. They're for the picking — only watch out that McCrae isn't doing a bit of picking at the same time.'

Then they sat in the shade for half an hour to recover. Both Rorke and Jay Key were still deaf from the gun blasts and were glad of the respite. After a time Peaches relieved Glamour, who came down and did her share of hugging. Rorke said, 'Another week, honey, and you'll be human — almost.' Glamour didn't mind now. These men were strong and resourceful; she was putting her faith in them for her salvation, and up to now they hadn't done badly. They could tease as much as they liked; she knew now they weren't being malicious with it.

Rorke said, 'Now what do we do?' Harry Carley had answered that question for himself a good time back and was sweating over his transmitter.

Jay thought for a while and then said, 'We've got to stay by the tank. How about putting in time trying to get that amphibian in order? We wouldn't dare risk a long voyage in her, but — well, you never know. Suppose that gun of yours goes out of action? We're back where we started; in that case I'd take a chance on making those islands way out west.'

Rorke said, 'It'd be a hell of a slim chance, I think.' But all the same he rose and climbed wearily back into the tank.

'Okay, Jay, we might as well work as do nothing.'

For a couple of hours, they worked steadily on the amphibian. Jay got working on the engine, though he said there wasn't much to do to it, while Rorke explored for weak places in the hull and screwed on plates of aluminum that he found on a scrap heap. Afterwards, he hoped to find some paint or pitch or something to waterproof the whole underwater surface. He wasn't impressed with his patching; he knew that after all this time out of water the vibration of the engines would tear the hull gradually apart at the seams. Still, as Jay said, they might be prepared to take any risk, shortly.

Once or twice, some of the women came across with messages from the nest. Apparently the trio had been joined by Nona McCrae now, and all were resting up from their recent shocks down by the lagoon, oblivious, apparently, to the fact that they could be seen from the water tower. Each time the women came they went to the fallen palm and brought back armfuls of nuts, some of which they opened for the benefit of the very hot and weary mechanics. They needed it.

Rorke told the women to be very careful. 'I know you're within sight of us, but for God's sake don't take any risks. McCrae wouldn't be any different with a woman.' He shuddered at the thought of one of these women falling into the hands of McCrae, the man who had been a specialist in brutality. Better for them to die first.

But McCrae wasn't seen all that morning. He'd had enough, evidently, for a while.

It was some time in the early afternoon. The sun was glistening in its intensity, the intense, near-tropical light blinding to their eyes. Under it the palms drooped their ragged edges as if it were more than they could stand, too. Only the distant blue sea looked sparklingly alive, but it held an invitation that none could use just yet.

Lucky Josie was up top, where the only cool breezes were to be found, keeping watch and dreaming about inch-thick steaks and mounds of brown roast potatoes with great rough hunks of bread piled all around. Solid food. Craving for it. Hating the coconut that she had to munch to try to allay the never-quietened pangs of hunger . . . the coconut that had seemed like manna to them such a short time ago.

In the hut with Harry Carley was the mighty-limbed Glamour, incongruously perched on top of the skeleton bicycle generator, her legs driving the pedals round effortlessly. She had her dress tucked up into another garment so as to give freedom of movement to her strong brown legs, and everyone was completely unconcerned about her appearance, for once in her camera-cradled life.

Harry was blaspheming steadily as improvisation after improvisation failed. He wasn't the plump Harry Carley of a few days back — now he was down to bone and muscle, and rapidly getting through the muscle at that.

Rorke had found some paint. It was in several colours, but he mixed it and produced a workmanlike grey-green and was now painting it onto the hull with a lump of hessian sacking that had survived the general decay in the graveyard. Inside the amphibian, spare, balding little Jay Key was going on enthusiasm alone. He was whacked, drugged with the frantic endeavour of the day and the awful, dulling weight of torrid sunshine that never let up for a second. But he was getting results with this engine. He could start it, though it was firing badly. Now he was licking it into shape and it was improving every minute in performance. The engine didn't worry him; it was that damned leaky bottom.

Peaches' job was to open coconuts and take them round as refreshment to the workers. It was a full-time job in that heat. Rorke calculated they were drinking at least a pint of coconut milk every quarter of an hour; they were losing so much in the way of perspiration. And he and Jay were dreaming of three-inch steaks.

There was a heavy, sultry peace. A quietness that hung like a mist over that low-lying island in that dazzling blue sea.

Peaches had gone to the fallen palm on the fringe of the bush. That was only a hundred yards or so away, within sight . . . safe enough.

And then she screamed. It rose out from the green brush, a sound that shocked because it told of the death that was within inches of her — a scream that tore through the mind like a coarse-bladed hacksaw dragging through soft brain itself.

Hearing it, horror gripped them. And then Josie was leaning over, shouting down to them, sobbing with grief because she was now seeing what she hadn't been able to see seconds before.

Peaches went on screaming — it went higher, sharply higher, then impossibly high. And then stopped as though a guillotine had sliced through the sound. There was a thrashing of weight and strength back among the green bushes, and then it receded and there was silence.

Rorke started to run towards the fallen palm, and then he stopped and stood, unable to decide for a moment on the right course of action. All he could think just then was, *Now it's Peaches. One by one we're all going . . . Only — why pick on poor old Peaches?* Poor feather-brained, lovely Peaches . . .

But those thoughts didn't help. He pulled himself together. It wasn't any good running blindly after the enemy, whichever it was. It wouldn't do Peaches any good to get in the way of a bullet, and there were two other women to think about.

He made decisions. He had only to point to the tank, and Jay was streaking across to it quite a bit faster than an Olympic champion. Esther was burning the ground across to the water tower, but when she got there Josie was coming quickly down. Harry came crashing across through the waste and junk by the collapsed huts.

Rorke raced over to the tank. 'Don't come down, Josie!' he shouted.

Josie stopped, thirty feet up on the narrow iron ladder. Her face was tear-streaked as she looked down, show-ing the agony of misery that racked her just then. She sobbed, 'Oh, Pat, it was

McCrae himself. He must have crept up through the bush — he must have been waiting for poor Peaches to walk into his arms. I should have noticed, only — ' She was bewildered. ' — he never seemed to leave the beach. He still seems to be there.'

Rorke said soothingly, 'Don't take on, Josie. McCrae's cunning. He must have guessed we were watching and left his jacket on a bush as a decoy. I shouldn't have let Peaches go into the bush.' He wheeled on Harry, coming up. 'Harry, you operate the tank gun.' He was glad he'd shown the works earlier that day to the radio man. 'You women stay up top irrespective of what happens.' Back to Harry again, a rough idea forming. 'Get Jay to go down the runway, then find a weak place on the neck and try to break through to the lagoon. Use your gun, make a noise — you won't catch them among these trees, but it should secure their attention and I might be able to do something.'

'Such as?'

'If Peaches is alive, I'm going to get her

away from that murdering swine. I don't know how I'll do it, but I know it can't be done from inside a tank.'

'You're going afoot?'

Rorke was picking up a piece of iron pipe and hefting it. He nodded.

Harry said, 'Good luck, Pat,' and then belted off to where the tank was already crabbing round on its duff tread. It came crashing across, splintering the fallen hut to matchwood, rearing mountainously as it breasted the slope on to Main Street. Then it was away in a deafening crescendo of acceleration and ponderously moving metal, dust blowing up, flames belching where they shouldn't have been, from the exhaust.

Rorke dived into the bush, circling so as to come out on to the lagoon beach away from where McCrae usually camped. After the first few paces caution prevailed and he went quietly, keeping watch and stopping at any suspicious movement or sound. He was still saying to himself, 'It doesn't help Peaches for me to stop some lead.' And McCrae was the kind of tactician to have set an ambush for the unwary.

But for once, McCrae didn't seem to have thought so far ahead. There was no trace of the big man or his companions anywhere. All the same, Rorke didn't relax his caution, and for that reason it took all of a quarter of an hour or more to cover the half-mile to the lagoon.

He was still deep in the bush when the distant roaring of the tank took on a deeper, rougher note. Then he heard the gun blast off. He wondered if Harry had spotted McCrae or if this were just a diversionary noise. It grew louder as he came farther up the east jaw of the spit round the lagoon. Once or twice he even heard the whistle of a madly rotating shell before it smashed into some palm tree or missed everything and whined out across the lagoon.

To Rorke, it sounded like war again. It must have been a chilling barrage of sound for McCrae and party to digest.

As it turned out, burdened as he was, McCrae couldn't have been much ahead of Rorke. Coming faster now because his progress was covered by that awesome battering as the tank fought its way through the trees, Rorke actually saw McCrae the moment he stepped out on to the beach.

He saw him go out into the open, heavy, lumbering, sweating, still wearing those business tycoon's glasses. Saw him stop as if some sight astounded him. Then he went forward.

Rorke risked everything in a swift race up to the fringe of bushes. The first thing he saw was big solid McCrae going rapidly down the beach, Peaches dragging behind as he towed her by one arm. She looked like an old coat . . . or a corpse. She wasn't conscious, anyway.

The next thing Rorke saw was a boat. It was standing a few yards off shore, a native craft. It looked a crazy, narrow craft, probably made from a hollowed-out tree trunk, and it had a kind of boom riding out at one side to balance it. There was a short mast and a square of dull brown sail.

Five natives were in the boat. Two wore tattered canvas jeans that looked like discarded G.I. clothing; the other three were clad only in loin cloths. All were naked on the upper part of their brown, nearly black bodies. Their faces were broad and prominent at the cheekbones, again nearly black, and their hair was crinkly and stood high off their heads. All had horizontal tribal scars across their faces, though at this moment they looked like very scared men.

Little Japanese Charlie was up to his waist in water, holding on to the outrigger. He was blinking behind his glasses, but the gun in his hand didn't waver from the natives, all the same.

Joe Gunter, the lines on his face so deep and marked by now that they appeared to have been seamed in with a branding iron, was holding the bow of the quaint craft. On the beach stood Nona. The third automatic was in her hand, but she held it down at her side, as if not even knowing it was in her hand. And her face, as she stared away across the lagoon at nothing, had the blankness of the windows of a forlorn, deserted house. Something had already gone from behind that face.

Jay was smashing his way down to the

beach, and the mighty revving roar filled the lagoon with echoes. Rorke knew what was going to happen, and all he thought was *Jay, you're wasting your time. We can't catch them now.*

But it was still madness to go rushing down to the water's edge and try to rescue Peaches . . .

Rorke heard Japanese Charlie shrill out above the clamour: 'They came sneaking in just after you left, Alec, but I got 'em.'

McCrae shouted: 'We can do with it — now!' He looked back towards the general direction of the noise from the tank. A tree crashed, and now Jay was so near to the beach that they saw it topple with its green head on the sand. It must have been startling to McCrae. Then McCrae shouted: 'We can't all go in it,' and raised the gun and fired twice. Two natives slumped into the water. One didn't make a sound and remained nearly submerged. The other had a shattered breast bone, but managed to crawl ashore, screaming. McCrae didn't even bother to turn round and look at him. After a few seconds the native slumped and Rorke, even from that distance, knew he was dead.

McCrae, his shirt black where the sweat stuck it to his broad back, waved his gun and said something sharply, and at once the three natives started to pull the sail round to catch the wind. McCrae climbed into the stern, watching the natives, the gun steady in his big hand, no longer as fat as it had been a few days before, nor as pale.

He said something to Japanese Charlie, who hoisted the limp figure of the now feebly stirring Peaches into the boat and then climbed in himself. Joe Gunter still held on to the bows. He shouted anxiously to McCrae, who jerked his gun impatiently. Rorke caught the words: 'Get in quick, if you're coming!' Spoken as though McCrae didn't give a damn if he didn't come.

Gunter shouted again, frantically, and pointed to Nona. McCrae snapped at him, but Gunter pulled the bow on to the beach, then ran across and towed his sister along by the hand. Rorke hadn't heard much, but he could guess what it all added up to. McCrae wouldn't have bothered about his wife if Joe Gunter hadn't gone and fetched her. Nona had served her purpose; now she could go. Perhaps back of that empty face she dimly realised it . . .

Jay pulled the tank round and suddenly smashed a road through the bush and came out on to the beach. The boat was shoving off, beginning to skim across the lagoon to the narrow sea entrance. Rorke came out and sat on the beach. Jay thundered up and then cut the engine.

Harry was going frantic up in the turret, his face begrimed from his gunnery. 'Pat, Pat,' he kept shouting, 'what is there we can do?'

Rorke said: 'Just now, nothing. They've got Peaches with them, so we can't just open fire and try to sink 'em. That's why he bothered to take her with them, I suppose.'

McCrae was sitting, massive and unemotional, with his arm holding Peaches upright. There was no affection in the embrace; it was intended to show the party on the beach that here was a hostage who would suffer whatever he and his party suffered.

So they watched them go out to sea.

12

The Amphibian

Rorke said: 'The only thing is we must risk the colander, Jay.'

'The amphibian?'

Rorke nodded. 'You and I will go. Harry must stay and finish his transmitter and look after the women. After all these years out of water she's sure to go under, but — '

'But we've got to try to rescue Peaches.' Little Jay didn't draw back.

They left the tank and trudged back to the tower. Both women came down to meet them. Jay quickly made his adjustments to the engine, Rorke dug up the biggest can he could find to act as a bailer, and then they started to move the vehicle down to the beach. It was running on the ruins of old tyres, and they were able to get it across the soft, sandy beach only by first laying down a carpet of palm

207

branches. But in the end it dipped its nose into the gentle waves of the blue sea and . . . floated.

Josie was crying again. She thought it was all her fault that Peaches had been kidnapped. They kept telling her that it could have happened with anyone on watch, but there was no soothing her. For now two more of the party were going . . .

Glamour showed real emotion for the first time, too. She looked big — a fine, handsome woman in her tattered finery. And the way she looked at them, they knew she was realising how much she had come to know and rely on them in these few short days.

Harry had to hold Josie up as they pushed off. He didn't say much, just 'Good luck.' But he must have been thinking unhappy thoughts. There had been fifteen people alive in that Constellation when it came down that day on this runway. Now only three remained; five had died, and more must die shortly.

The engine started, and they pulled round to the lagoon entrance and then set course to the dim line that was the distant island from which the natives seemed to have come. Tahao itself grew smaller — the three forlorn figures on the beach tinier and tinier until they could no longer be seen.

After an hour, they spotted the sail of the native craft and changed course to come up with it. And it was only then that Jay said: 'What do we do when we get up to them, Pat?'

Rorke shook his head. McCrae still had guns — and a hostage. He said wearily: 'We'll see when we come up with the boat.'

His big worry just now was the increasing leakage of water into the amphibian. The pump was doing its best to keep the bilge tank free, but for the last half-hour he had had to assist by baling. And now it was becoming obvious that the water was gaining in spite of the combined effort. It was for that reason that they were crawling along so slowly, at no more than three or four knots. Rorke was sure that any faster speed would set up a vibration that would split them right open and let the engine drop out.

Tahao was still more prominent than the island ahead when the amphibian cruised level with the native sailing craft, though beyond pistol range.

McCrae sat and watched, Peaches white and terrified by his side. The three natives didn't know what to make of it, and were covertly watching while they handled the sail. Joe Gunter had the appearance of a man who wouldn't do much now, not even if it was to save his life, but Japanese Charlie hadn't changed at all. He leaned back, cross-legged, talking talking, talking. Talking all the time to McCrae, arguing about something, hair-splitting, unconcerned that McCrae didn't bother to make it a duologue.

And Nona sat and watched her husband. Just sat and watched.

Rorke kept looking across, but he didn't stop baling. The sweat rolled off him, though the heat of the day was now past by a few hours. Jay watched the water level and wondered how long it would be before it got at the engines. Already it was inches over the floor boards. He took over baling for a time to give Rorke a rest. They were maintaining a distant circle round the slow-tacking native boat.

Resting there, it gave Rorke time to think things out. At last he sighed, and said: 'You know what I think, Jay? Another hour and we'll be completely waterlogged. She won't sink, with these air tanks, but she won't move.'

Jay wiped the pouring sweat that came so easily with exertion and said: 'In which case, we'll have followed them for nothing. They'll get away after all.'

Rorke looked across at the bobbing, frail-looking sailing craft. 'Yeah. That's about it, Jay. So . . . '

Jay nodded comprehendingly. 'So if there's anything we can do, let's do it now, huh?'

Rorke sat upright behind the wheel. 'That's about it, Jay. God knows there's little we can do, with Peaches sitting there and us without arms. But — well, we've got to risk things. There's no future for Peaches, anyway, with McCrae holding on to her.'

Rorke revved the engine a little. Jay stopped his frantic baling and said: 'What're you going to do, Pat?' because he could see that Rorke had some desperate plan by the way his face was furrowed with anxiety.

Rorke pulled the wheel round and rose. 'Heaven help me, about all we can do, Jay. Look, you take the wheel. Rev up a bit and ram that craft broadside. I'll watch for Peaches and go in after her if I can't pull her aboard, so you watch out for both of us in the water.'

'What about the others?'

'They've just got to take a chance. If they all go into the water, we'll just circle and pick them up — if they're still on top by the time we get round.'

Jay said: 'The natives'll be all right, but . . . Nona McCrae? Poor woman, she's suffered enough for marrying that bastard.'

Rorke said: 'Jay, we've got to rescue Peaches. She's done no harm to anyone. She won't live if we don't make an effort, so take your choice — Nona or Peaches.'

Jay said: 'Peaches. But we'll do what we

can for that poor crackbrain.'

Rorke said: 'Right. Keep under cover and step on it, Jay. And let's pray that after the crash the damned thing holds together long enough for us to get back to Tahao.'

The amphibian gallantly tried to make speed, but with that weight of water dragging it low, it was slow in accelerating. Rorke realised it too late, realised that when they hit the boat they would come on it without any great speed, and that was vital to their plan.

Peering over the tiny covered bow, he saw McCrae and Charlie jump to their feet in alarm as they spotted the manoeuvre. One of the natives suddenly gabbled something and immediately the three dropped over the side. McCrae didn't see them go; he was firing with that little automatic.

Jay knew they weren't going fast enough, either, and he shouted in panic: 'What'll we do, Pat?'

Rorke just jerked back: 'Keep going. We'll sink it, anyway.' But both knew their cards were played out, knew exactly what would happen . . .

They came in so slowly that even big McCrae got aboard in one wild leap before the amphibian crashed into the fragile native craft; Charlie and Joe Gunter hung on for a moment to the gunwale before the weight of the amphibian sent the mast heeling over and the craft sinking under them. Then they clambered on board. Nona also got aboard. No one actually saw her do it, but later, when they turned, she was there, sitting, with her hair blowing, on one of the side seats.

Rorke knew that his plan had miscarried, but there was no turning back. He started to swing at McCrae jumping over, saw Peaches' white face within arm's reach, changed his mind and grabbed her as the water poured over her. When he pulled her over the side, he saw that McCrae was standing forward, his tiny automatic covering the boat. McCrae was in command again . . .

Rorke lowered Peaches on to the flooded deck, picked up the big baling can in the same movement and hurled it at McCrae, risking all . . . and nothing.

Because he knew he was going to die, anyway, within seconds. As he hurled the can, he flung himself forward in a dive that landed him flat in the wet of the deck forward.

McCrae blazed off and hit the can. The can seemed to halt in mid-air, just at the point of his gun, and then drop to the deck. McCrae fired and tore a lump out of the back of Rorke's neck, and then Rorke had him by a massive leg and smashed him back against the gunwale.

A shot cracked out back of him — one shot. But it didn't come his way.

There was no time for niceties. McCrae was strong, and that arm was already coming round to blow Rorke's head off. Rorke heaved on the leg and McCrae went over the side and into the water. When he came up, he was still wearing his glasses, but he'd lost his gun.

But there were still two guns behind him . . .

When he turned, he saw Charlie opening his mouth to scream. His right arm was shattered, and blood was gushing down his hand. In the water at his feet was his flat little automatic. Rorke was in time to see Nona's foot go out and hook it towards her, and then he saw the wisp of smoke from her automatic.

Joe Gunter, face working as his old fear came mounting up, shouted: 'My God, Nona, what did you want to shoot Charlie for?'

But Nona didn't say anything to him. She was looking round at her husband, swimming up behind. He had thrown his glasses away, and now his face, suddenly seeming big and bare and unclothed because it was the first time Rorke had seen him without glasses, looked terrible. The sort of face that many an obstinate American must have seen as he was dying . . .

Rorke said harshly: 'Go pick those boys up first,' indicating the three natives who were clinging to their overturned craft. Jay turned the wheel. Behind, in the water, McCrae shouted angrily. He didn't know what had happened to Japanese Charlie.

Rorke assisted Peaches onto a seat, but all the time he was maneuvering towards

Nona. Now there was only one gun aboard that was serviceable; whoever held that held the lives of all in his or her hands. He had to get it from Nona, one way or another.

The natives climbed into the sinking amphibian. They were suspicious, uncertain. Rorke shoved the perforated baling can into one of their hands and said: 'Bail, brother; it's better for all of us.' And got another couple of steps nearer towards Nona.

Jay turned from the wheel, and said: 'Now what?'

He was circling; McCrae was falling behind. McCrae was shouting, furious, bellowing orders.

Rorke took one more pace and started to turn. Nona said: 'Don't. I wouldn't want to shoot you.' And he saw that the gun was pointing towards him and the hand was steady. So he went and sat forward with Peaches and Jay.

When he was seated, he asked: 'What do you want us to do, Mrs. McCrae?' And it seemed curious to call anyone missus in those circumstances. She didn't answer. She was looking into the face of her husband, twenty yards astern. Rorke said: 'Don't you want us to pick up your husband?' She had her back to him now, and he could have got the gun, possibly. She shook her head.

And Rorke understood. There is always a last straw. Perhaps that had come back on the beach when McCrae hadn't been bothered about taking her with him . . .

He turned to Jay and said: 'You keep going for Tahao as fast as you can. I'll keep 'em bailing.'

Jay said: 'The others?'

Rorke said: 'We can forget about them all now, I think. Now we can manage the situation . . . '

The sinking amphibian crawled slowly through the blue sea as the sun lowered behind them, rich and red and still warm to their backs. As it went, the boat pushed up a long bow wave that seemed to dissolve only on the horizon that was so near, here close to the water level. And every minute the weight grew and the engines laboured, and their speed decreased until they weren't making more than a couple of knots, perhaps less.

But they were still going too fast for McCrae. They saw him following behind; once he must have been a good swimmer. For a time he almost seemed to keep pace with them, and then gradually he dropped back, farther and farther, but he still kept on after them, as if unbelieving that his wife and friends wouldn't be able to do something for him.

But they couldn't, and didn't. Nona sat back in the stern, hunched and watching, her eyes never leaving the big moon face that rose wetly above the dancing waves.

In time he must have understood. Then he started to waste his breath in shouting after them, though they couldn't tell what he said. The water got into his throat and his voice came up in a choking, gasping roar, and then he stopped shouting. After this, he swam on but feebly for another ten minutes, and then they saw him go under. He must have swallowed a lot of water. He came up for a minute and then went under again. They never saw Alec McCrae after that.

Nona stood up and watched for a

minute, and then she stepped over the side. There wasn't an expression on her face as she pulled the trigger for the last time. It was now completely empty.

They didn't stop to pick her up. They knew she was dead before she hit the water. People usually are when they blow holes through their skulls.

No one spoke. Rorke made them all take turns at bailing. The island looked quite big when the engine spluttered and stopped. He made them start paddling with floorboards, but they didn't seem to make headway, and finally night came.

They sat perched round the edge of the boat while the water came to within nine inches of the top and stayed there all night. No one spoke much. Joe Gunter kept moaning and holding his stomach until Japanese Charlie lost his temper and snapped: 'If you'd the guts of your sister, you'd go over the side, too.' But Joe Gunter hadn't that kind of guts, and just went on moaning and doing nothing about it.

Japanese Charlie tried to justify all that had happened in a lengthy speech to

Rorke, but little Jay got tired first and shut him up by saying: 'Listen, you lousy renegade, I'll kick your larynx in with pleasure to shut you up. So — *shut up!*' And Jay would have done it, and liked the excuse, so Charlie sat back and thought out arguments for when he appeared before a court representing the citizens of the United States of America.

All night they drifted. When dawn came, quickly lighting the sky, they found themselves less than a quarter of a mile from the island. A quarter of a mile — and in their condition there wasn't one who could swim that distance, unless it was the natives.

They got out their improvised paddles, and all took turns, but their progress was so slow that it was a long time before they knew they were making headway. Long before this, the women came down to the beach, waving to them; and when they saw Rorke and Jay, and then Peaches, all waving cheerfully back, they danced with joy.

Harry didn't come for a while, but when finally he came down to the beach, they felt that he had achieved something that was to his satisfaction.

It was nearly noon when they finally came into the shallows and were able to wade ashore. Josie and Esther came waist deep to greet them. Three glad natives and two depressed white men saw them join up.

Little Jay, big Pat Rorke . . . tearful, smiling Josie, blonde, happy Peaches . . . mighty-limbed, glamorous Esther Van Kass, laughing with them . . . and good old Harry waiting with drink on the beach.

They climbed out through the surf, linked in one long joyful line. They had been through hell and come through; they knew what comradeship meant. Now a time of peace was to come for them . . .

Out from the eastern horizon came a four-engined U.S. aircraft. That was what Harry had called up that morning. In a matter of hours they would be on their way out from Tahao, on their way to the dull, humdrum of their normal existence. And all anyone could say was: 'Lead me to it — fast!'

We do hope that you have enjoyed reading this large print book.

Did you know that all of our titles are available for purchase?

We publish a wide range of high quality large print books including:
Romances, Mysteries, Classics
General Fiction
Non Fiction and Westerns

Special interest titles available in large print are:
The Little Oxford Dictionary
Music Book, Song Book
Hymn Book, Service Book

Also available from us courtesy of Oxford University Press:
Young Readers' Dictionary
(large print edition)
Young Readers' Thesaurus
(large print edition)

For further information or a free brochure, please contact us at:
Ulverscroft Large Print Books Ltd.,
The Green, Bradgate Road, Anstey,
Leicester, LE7 7FU, England.
Tel: (00 44) **0116 236 4325**
Fax: (00 44) **0116 234 0205**

Other titles in the
Linford Mystery Library:

SHERLOCK HOLMES: JOURNEYS BY TRAIN

N. M. Scott

In his capacity as a consulting detective, Sherlock Holmes and his companion Dr Watson invariably find themselves travelling a good deal by train, and it is this which links the seemingly disparate events in one of the most fraught episodes in Holmes's career. A 'wheelchair mob' plans a series of daring gem heists, and ghosts are allegedly committing theft! Amid murder, poisoning and séances, someone is also threatening the faithful landlady, Mrs Hudson. Can Holmes get to the bottom of the mystery and bring the criminals to justice?

CASEY AND THE LOST BOYS

Geraldine Ryan

As DI Casey Clunes investigates the whereabouts of a missing volunteer, the suspicious behaviour of a group of schoolboys begins to interrupt not only her work, but her home life too . . . In *The Other Diana*, a teacher reveals a long-kept secret, leading to the reopening of a twenty-year-old unsolved case involving a murdered girl . . . And in *After Phoebe*, Vonny is forced to take a job at Oxford University and confront the darkness of her past. But now, she feels the presence of something far more threatening than her memories . . .

WHO WAS SYLVIA?

Carol Cail

After Maxey releases the body of a stranger called Sylvia for burial, she is determined to publish an obituary for the woman in her newspaper, *The Blatant Regard*. As she investigates further into Sylvia's life, Maxey is also intrigued by a man's death in a mattress store fire, just half a block from her own apartment. But when Maxey disappears on Halloween, it's up to her business partner Scotty and her lover, Fire Marshall Calen Taylor, to sort the tricks from the treats as she tangles with undisguised death.